5/8/2024

Thank you Mike
I hope you enjoy
the adventure

check
the
back

SPACE AGE CHRONICLES
MARS

JOSHUA LEVI

ISBN (Print): 978-1-09837-948-3
ISBN (eBook): 978-1-09837-949-0

Thank you to my friends and family who have supported my ideas and helped inspire me and push me to get this done.

CHAPTER 1
The Verdict

United Earth Supreme Court of Extreme Crimes,
Kansas City, Kansas

"Lieutenant Colonel Eric Cartwright, before I read the verdict of this court, do you have anything to say in your defense?"

With broad shoulders and a scowl that demands attention, Cartwright is a towering leader with eyes like steel that slice through anyone. .

"Those people were all guilty of trying to destabilize the world government! I did what nobody else would to protect our planet from further terrorism! If anyone is guilty, it's all of you for trying to stop me! You've doomed yourselves!"

"That is out of line Colonel Cartwright!" exclaimed the Judge. "You massacred women and children with no such ties to terrorist cells. The evidence showed that there was no threat in those areas. You were under no authority to even be in those areas. This court finds you and your battalion guilty of crimes against humanity."

Eric's face turned from shock at the announcement to horror at the words "of your entire battalion".

He exclaimed, "Please, your honor! Condemn me if you must, but not my men. They are good soldiers just following my orders. While I disagree with you, I am their leader and to be solely held accountable for their actions."

The judge looked back at him with disgust. "Your men are just as guilty for following you. The ends do not justify the means, Colonel Cartwright, and in our society, all have the ability to make the right or wrong choice. Many of your battalion saw you make the wrong choice and rightly chose to turn you in and leave your battalion. Those that stayed with you are just as guilty as you are.

"Those captured with you will receive a lesser punishment than you. Before I hand you your sentence, I will allow you this one courtesy of knowing the fate of those who are currently in custody."

Whispers in the audience were getting louder and the judge cleared his throat signaling the audience to fully silence themselves before continuing.

Looking at the display in front of him, he listed the names of all those incarcerated finishing with, "These members of the 42nd Rangers also known as the Hawkeye Battalion are sentenced to ten years at Alcatraz Island Penitentiary for rehabilitation. At the end of this sentence, if rehabilitation and reunification into our armed forces is deemed not possible, they will be transferred to the 10 Hygeia Maximum Security Penal Colony."

Judge Richardson continues with disgust, nearly spitting the title, "Colonel Eric Cartwright, this court sentences you to life without parole in the 10 Hygeia Maximum Security Penal Colony upon its completion. Until then, you will be held at the Mars Maximum Penitentiary."

Cartwright jumps to his feet in outrage while thunderous applause echoes around him in the courtroom and around the globe.

Judge smashes his gavel against the block resting on the bench. "Order! I will have order in the court until I am finished!" When silence finally falls upon the ecstatic courthouse, the judge continues.

"The remainder of your battalion, once found and taken into custody, they will be joining you. For not turning themselves in when they could have." Cartwright was on his feet once more in anger now yelling at the judge. Richardson, ignoring him, stood up himself, assembling his belongings on the bench and waved to the officers on either side of the bench. "Bailiffs, take this man out of my sight. This court is adjourned!" With that, Judge Richardson walked away and into his back office. He left Cartwright screaming, the court in an uproar of applause, and the sounds of celebration that could be heard around the world.

"No! No you can't do this! I was protecting you people! I'm no criminal! I'll have my revenge, yet!" Cartwright yelled as the three bailiffs forcibly pulled him out of the court house, bound for temporary detention cell until his flight to Mars.

* * *

Meanwhile somewhere on Luna...

Quietly content, Major John Capperman sits alone in the commander's quarters of a secret base. Smiling and contemplating how well things had gone according to plan. Knowing things never go according to plan, it brought great pleasure thinking about it.

Phase one of his commanding officer's plan had just been completed as expected. Lunar Base Six, a small military intelligence base on the dark side of the moon, had easily been captured with all but the highest-skilled personnel killed or "persuaded" to work for the Hawkeye Battalion. Those senior officers were currently being interrogated by the unit's intelligence gathering expert, Lieutenant Jack Harvey, and disposed of afterwards. Once that was finished the Hawkeye's five spaceships; two interceptor shuttles, two fighter escorts, and troop transport, as well as the facility's three fighters and single carrier were being prepared for phase two: rescue the unit's leader en route to Mars.

Capperman had been Eric Cartwright's best friend growing up and loyal second in command since he was assigned to this unit eight years earlier. Life on Earth had certainly changed in that time.

The "United Earth" was far from United. In actuality it was more like it had always been. There was the U.N. and their biased nations dealing with all the third world nations and terrorists. But the U.N. felt once they established the Lunar Colonies and began building those Mars colonies, the interstellar community would be better run, with Earth united under one planetary government with individual countries acting more like states.

There were the colonies. The Lunar and Martian Colonies, as well as multiple space stations and fleets of various types of ships had created tons of business and military strength for America, Russia, and China. That was until they were forced into sharing everything with the other nations of the world. If the Earth was to be united through its extraplanetary properties, its interplanetary society should be reaping the benefits as a whole.

Warehouses were everywhere, importing resources from Luna, Mars and asteroids towed near to Earth. Earth's resources were being depleted like never before while the colonies were being built. Now with almost nothing left on the blue planet, the colonies were selling Earth what they mined at a premium price because of the cost of entering the atmosphere. Even fuels were cheaper off-world. Compared to the extravagant wealth of its colonies, Earth was akin to a third world country.

Capperman and Cartwright, both growing up in D.C. as part of military families, had seen all of this up close. They soon saw America as becoming dependent on its services to keep afloat. Cartwright wanted to take them out. Make Earth for Earth again and Capperman was right by his side along with the majority of the Hawkeye Battalion.

Capperman was going over the events that had led them to this place, this day, when his comm crackles to life.

"Major Capperman, please come in!" Sergeant McAllen's voice carried into the major's ears.

"Capperman, here, go ahead, McAllen."

"Sir, we have just received word that Colonel Cartwright has been sentenced to Mars Maximum and will be departing in 36 hours from Obama Spaceport

outside of Chicago. They will be refueling at Exxon Station before jumping to Mars." The young man's voice was calm but urgent.

The battalion was anxiously awaiting this moment. McAllan, the bright, Montanan boy, badly wanted his commanding officer back, feelings Capperman still picked up on through the transmission despite the kid's attempted stoicism.

Ships make orbital "jumps" by accelerating in orbit of the moon and breaking out of orbit at 12Gs in the direction of their destination. The velocity shortens the duration of the trip by half. In order to properly intercept the transport, they would have to stop it before Cartwright enters Luna's orbital jump trajectory.

"Understood. Does Yaslov have a time for us to leave so that we can intercept?" Capperman said.

"*Not yet, sir, he says he can't make a proper calculation until they have lifted off from Earth. Too many variables can cause the lift-off to be delayed, so it's best to wait for them to be in the air and leaving Earth's atmosphere before making the calculation. But it should be about eight hours from lift-off to Exxon Station, and we should leave when they get to Exxon.*" Seeing where the wind was blowing, Earth's major oil companies were among the first to invest in the Mars colonies.

"I have a better idea." Capperman's lips turned into a full grin as a new plan unwound in his head. "Let's leave to get to Exxon Station just before they arrive. We'll take over Exxon Station and rescue the Colonel when they refill. We'll also capture the transport."

McAllen's macho pretense suddenly fell away; he was shocked Capperman wanted to radically change the strategy.

"*But sir that wasn't the plan that Colonel Cartwright laid out for us.*" The words awkwardly stumbled out of the sergeant's mouth."

"He didn't know where he would be refueling. We do."

Abruptly, a new voice enters the conversation. "*Major, I don't think he will be going to Exxon Station.*"

The heavy Russian accent came from Lieutenant Eugene Yaslov. "*This is too out in the open, Exxon is a commercial refueling station. I would put 1,000 credits that they actually send out two transports; one to Exxon as a diversion and the other one to Automated Refueling Station Beta.*"

"*It does sound like something that they would do, especially since they know we'll be trying to set him free,*" McAllen's voice returned.

"Good point, both of you," Capperman said. "At least they don't know where we are, or even that we're definitely off Earth. Okay, Yaslov, where are we intercepting them then?"

"I'm glad you asked me that, sir; I have plotted the best place for us to intercept them just before they enter the Lunar Jump Orbit. We will have only a few minutes to disable their engines, board, get the colonel, and leave to head back here."

"One flaw with your plan, Yaslov. We want to capture the transport for our purposes, not let it fall into Luna's orbit."

"Don't worry, Major, I have just finished installation of grappling guns onto our transport. We can tow the ship with us; and they'll still be trying to figure out what happened!"

Capperman could hear the smile in Yaslov's voice and couldn't help but offer a chuckle of his own. "Okay, we leave in 44 hours. Get some sleep and be prepared."

"Yes, sir!" the voices replied in unison and clicked off. Silence returns to the room, but it's only a temporary stay.

CHAPTER 2
The Anniversary

Frontier Colony, Mars

I t was a typical Martian day when Jacob Fallok awoke with his wife, Doctor Juliet Fallok slumbering peacefully beside him. He looked at her and smiled, this was no typical Martian day. Today was a beautiful and magnificent Martian day. He slowly made his way out of the bed trying to keep from waking his darling wife. He crept across the room, slipped through the doorway and tiptoed down the stairs to the kitchen. It was their 30th Anniversary and he wanted to make it perfect, starting with breakfast in bed.

Jacob turned on the monitor in the kitchen and tuned to the news for his morning fix. Approaching the fridge, Jacob queued the ingredients for his great grandfather's recipe of pancakes. As he was preparing the time honored tradition, he fell into his thoughts. Every year he looks forward to his anniversary, it was the same day as his grandparents. Three days after his 10th anniversary, is when that fateful day occurred.

His father, Joshua Fallok, was a wealthy business man on Earth who'd devoted his life to making money in the hopes of one day establishing a colony on Mars to help further the scientific and technological aspects of humanity in addition to help solve the growing population problems.

Joshua had sacrificed himself to save the rest of the colony; four years into the colonization when a safety hatch blew and caused a crack on the outer dome of one of the original Bio-Dome Facilities that housed the colony. He went into the compartment to seal it up from the inside preventing a complete breach of the dome and saving the 2,463 inhabitants.

Jacob was heating the pan for the pancakes when the reporter's words managed to penetrate his thoughts, capturing his attention.

"Reports show that Colonel Cartwright was working with Prime Minister Vritlianese to commit genocide in Senegal and Western Sahara. After the massacre in Kuba, Mali by Colonel Cartwright both were captured and charged with crimes against humanity. After months of trials, both Vritlianese and Cartwright were found guilty and sentenced to Life on 10 Hygeia. The two will be sharing a transport from Obama Spaceport in Chicago to Mars Maximum at eight a.m. tomorrow morning, local time. The remaining members of the Hawkeye Battalion that are still at large are believed to be hiding out somewhere in Mali after an

attack at the Kali Military Base. There a small military plane was taken by a group of commandos believed to be them."

Jacob stood there stunned even as the next story came and went. They were sending these butchers to his home as a punishment. He thought to himself. Oblivious to everything around him including his burning butter.

"In related news, the influx of jobs by the 10 Hygeia and AB Mining operation has helped the global economy exponentially. Wall Street is continuing on its rally and the NASDAQ is up 800 points upon opening after the verdict on Cartwright and Vritlianese was made."

Suddenly aware of the smell of the butter, Jacob quickly moved the pan to the sink and washed it to start over while still listening to the reporter in the background.

"Here is UE President Sadie Weisman at a Press Conference held immediately following the verdict of the two men."

"Today marks a historic day for our planet. Every century must face a trial of good versus evil. These two criminals are our evil and we have been triumphant against them.

We are now closer than ever before to a fully united planet in the name of peace. I applaud the honorable Judge Mathew Richardson on doing a commendable job with such a sad and heart breaking case. And to the Jurors who had the terrible responsibility of listening and seeing all of the evidence brought to them. Thank you all for your hard work."

Now that his pan was washed and he was past his shock he knew he needed to call his best friend, head of the colony's defenses. As he went to restart breakfast...

"Time for our daily launch watch here on Mars—"

"Call Brigadier General Joseph Ferguson at Geraldo Base," Jacob said, interrupting the anchor and causing the monitor to freeze momentarily before switching to a picture of the symbol for the Martian Defense Force. As he waited, Jacob pondered what he had just seen. Then a familiar voice came on the line.

Jacob peered at the dark skinned, bald man with a charming smile. His eyes immediately brightened at the sight of his longtime friend.

"Jacob, good morning; to what do I owe this early call?" Joseph opened excitedly.

"Good morning, Joe," Jacob said, slightly tired. "Have you seen today's news feed?"

"Yeah." Joe's tone losing some of its excitement, he continued, *"I have a meeting with Dustin in a couple hours to go over his security plans for the two new cells we're making for them at Mars Max. You want to come for the meeting? I'm sure you can give him a few pointers."*

Seeing this conversation could last a while longer than he first thought, Jacob shut the flame down so as not to burn more butter and took a seat with his coffee as he continued. "Only if you want me to. I don't need to be stepping on anybody's shoes. But these are the two most dangerous men of our lifetimes."

Joe had clasped his hands together just below his chin. His head leaning almost onto his hands, he slowly nodded in agreement. *"Well, this is why I'd like you here, too."*

Jacob put his hands up in playful surrender. "Okay, okay, I'll come," Jacob said, smiling slightly and lowering his hands as he continued. "Oh, and speaking of meetings, did Rob email you about a meeting today?"

Joe gave a small chuckle as he confirmed. *"Yeah, he got to you, too, eh? It looks like we have a busy day ahead of us."*

Jacob shook his head in disagreement. "No, just these two meetings, then I plan on having a nice relaxing day with my wife."

Joe was momentarily confused until realization came over him and he lit up again. *"Oh, that's right! Thirty years today."* Joe gave a quick laugh and then sighed as he began to reminisce. *"Wow. You damn lucky fool. I wish I'd had as much time with Candice."* Candice was Joe's wife who'd died a few years ago while visiting family on Earth.

"I know, we all do, she was great," Jacob replied, as he thought back to her delicious baked goods. "I haven't had Gingersnap cookies that good since."

Joe was in a full blown laugh now as Jacob continued.

"Juliet's great and all but she can't bake to save her life." As he'd said that Joe's eyes went wide, and his laugh turned down to a wide mischievous grin across his narrow face. The next thing Jacob knew, there was a sound of a foot tapping behind him...then he heard it.

"Ahem?" Jacob turned his head slowly, looking at the kitchen entrance he saw her. The most beautiful woman in his universe. Leaning on the door frame, wearing a violet bathrobe with the initials JF, her long brown hair resting lazily on her shoulders, and bright green eyes piercing at the two men; she gave a stern but mysterious slant of a smile before stepping another foot into the room enriched with the wonderful aroma of fresh coffee. This was his wife Juliet, who'd heard that whole last part and Jacob knew it by that smile, and her tapping foot. The room was silent though for a moment, Jacob captivated by the beauty of his wife. Still just as gorgeous as the day he had met her. Joe stupefied and wanting to break the silence.

"Good morning, Juliet." Joe grinned. *"Happy Anniversary!"*

"Good morning Joe, thank you," she said, allowing a full smile out before continuing. "Do you mind if I steal my husband for a little while or are you two still reminiscing on my skills as a housewife?" Jacob and Joe couldn't help but grin at Juliet for that.

"Go ahead, Jacob; I'll see you in a couple hours." With that Joe hung up before Jacob had a chance to say another word. He was quickly on his feet, coffee in hand ready to kiss his lovely wife.

"Good morning, honey. Happy anniversary," Jacob said with a big grin as he walked over to kiss her. She gave him a nice peck on the cheek as she stole his cup of coffee and walked around the kitchen island to the breakfast table.

"Good morning, Jacob. So what was all that about, besides my baking skills, that is?" she said in a mocking voice between sips.

"Oh, not much, they've convicted Cartwright and Bali Whatever—" Jacob said as he sat next to her with a fresh cup of coffee.

"Vritlianese," she corrected him.

"You know I can't pronounce that. Anyway, they sentenced them to Life at 10 Hygeia. Hence more criminals are going to be joining our nice little piece of paradise."

"Oh, yay," she said sarcastically.

"My feelings precisely; so I have a meeting with the Mayor, Dustin, and Joe in a couple hours to deal with accommodations for our new guests. And then Rob wants to meet with Joe and me afterwards about something or other."

"So you have a busy day today, huh?" She said feigning hurt feelings.

"No, no, just these two meetings and I promise it'll be all us for the rest of the day. I made reservations at your favorite restaurant tonight," Jacob said with a big grin.

"Uh huh, so what time should I expect you?" She said, completely void of emotion as she picked up her tablet and started looking at notes.

"Honey, don't act like this. It's only 7:30. I should be done by noon. We can even have lunch together; go to the spa and the gym. See a movie? We just got a new one in yesterday... um, what was it called?" Talking fast and panicky, only she could get him like this.

"Jacob, it's ok. Finish making breakfast and I'll see you when you're done with Rob. I need to go do some shopping with Melissa and check in with Kevin at the lab."

"Ok, breakfast is almost done anyways," he said as he started pouring the pancakes onto the cold pan. Then realizing he'd goofed again, he went to wash the pan again as Juliet laughed.

CHAPTER 3
The Plan

Obama Spaceport, Earth

The trip from Kansas City to Chicago was long, bumpy, and annoying thanks to the guards whom he was sure were ordered to make life as difficult as possible without harming their prisoner. No alone time, not even any peace and quiet to contemplate his next move. He couldn't really blame the guards for doing their job; he would have done the same if he was in their position. Still though, he was a superior officer so he would make them pay later.

The van finally arrived and he could hear the guards coming around back. They opened the doors. He had no idea what time it was, only that it had been pitch black for the last few hours. The bright light of the morning sun was blinding after that, but at least he now knew it must be around 0600. This was his last Earth sunrise for the foreseeable future, and it was beautiful.

"Okay, Cartwright, time for your trip. Enjoy this sunrise, it'll be your last. Now out," one of his guards said.

As the former Colonel stood up and stepped out of the van, he took in a deep breath of fresh air, another soon to be memory.

"Why, thank you all for that grand gesture, I shall remember this sunrise for the rest of my life, as well as each of you," Cartwright said with a mischievous grin and air of confidence to his voice. "Well, we mustn't let my shuttle wait; I don't want to be late for a very important date now do I?" And with that, the prisoner and his entourage of guards boarded the prison transport and headed directly to the rear holding cells.

As they walked past the row of almost empty cells, the guards ushered him past a few of the occupied cells. These were rift raft here for savage murders, terrorism or other lifetime sentences. As he passed each one, he took a moment to acknowledge them with a charismatic smirk. This is going to be a fun trip, he thought to himself.

His cell was small and cramped, located at the back of the room, far from all but one of the occupied cells. Looking around his new accommodations, he noted that it was barely long enough to lie down on the bed; and barely wide enough for the only other piece of furniture, a toilet. Of course there were seat belts for it all. Once the former soldier entered his cell, the guard shut the door. All of the cells were made out of transparent durable plastic to allow for full transparency with the guards and prisoners as well as the low cost and weight.

Due to the already high cost of this transport ship, only six of its class had been built, three for Earth, one for Luna, and two for Mars. Though with this transport, this ship would be remaining on Mars for use of Mars maximum, once 10 Hygeia was completed. It was quite a beautiful ship, and he was really going to enjoy taking it over.

"Ah, Colonel Cartwright, how nice it is to see you again. A pity it must be in this setting," said the dark man with a thick Mande dialect in the next cell.

Eric took a moment to look at his new neighbor, eyeing his long time accomplice, with thick dark hair and large gut. "The same could be said of you, Mr. Prime Minister," replied Cartwright, with a smile when he spat out the now defunct title.

"You forget, Eric," Bali seethed angrily. "Your government has stripped me of my title, now I'm simply just Bali."

Just then, an announcement came in over the PA system, *"This is your captain speaking. Major Gordon to all hands onboard, buckle in and prepare for departure, we leave in T minus five minutes. Gordon out."*

The two prisoners looked at each other. "Looks like we're really leaving for Mars. Have you ever been there, Eric?" Bali inquired as he strapped in. Eric responded in the negative and Bali continued, "I've never even been into space, if you can believe it."

"Well, Bali, you were a prime minister of a third world country. You had no way of leaving the planet or any reason to," Eric replied matter-of-factly.

"Yes, Eric, you are right, as usual," sighed the former PM.

The guards headed out to their take off seats in the galley and the two men finished strapping themselves into their harnesses. The guards didn't care about checking that all the prisoners were secure. It would be suicide to not follow the directions. A few moments later the ship shook as it began its liftoff from Earth. Less than five minutes later, they were weightless and in space.

Underneath their cots were standard issue magnetic boots to allow people to stay grounded. Once it was safe to unbuckle, Cartwright went straight for the boots while Bali decided to take the moment to enjoy floating around, until he got queasy and discovered space sickness.

Five minutes after that, only twenty minutes into their Journey, a greenish former-prime minister had his magnetic boots on and was sitting in a room full of his own vomit. Cartwright, who was laughing this whole time, abruptly ceased once the vomit began seeping in through the talking holes between the cell's walls. At this point the guards finally came in, wearing space suits and laughing as they escorted the two men to a cabin to clean up and wait until the cell block was cleaned and sanitized. Due to their distance from the rest of the prisoners, they were the only ones who had to vacate the area.

Though no guards were in the room with them, they were under lock and away from the cameras and free to talk.

"So, what's the plan of escape?" asked Bali.

Eric began to grin. "Escape? What makes you think I have a plan? Where would we go? We have become encased by inhospitable surroundings for the rest of our lives with nowhere to escape to." Eric was toying with Bali and gaging his reaction with both amusement and annoyance. Bali was a man who could constantly try Eric's patience with his lack of understanding subtly.

"Oh, come now, Eric. If you had no plan for escape, why arrange for your men to head into space during your trial?"

Eric tried to hide a smirk at that thought. He and his men had spent months obtaining a small fleet of black market ships to escape Earth with instructions to head to a secret base on Luna, and Bali's men had created a nice diversion hijacking some planes in Mali wearing the colors of Hawkeye. "A point well taken, Bali, which reminds me. Thank you for your help."

"Thank you for your help?" Bali started, a look of shock on his face. Eric watched in amusement as Bali changed from surprise to upset and continued. "That's it? What about our escape?"

Eric smiled, placed a comforting hand on his "friend" and attempted to calm him through some enlightenment. "Patience, my friend; let us just say we aren't going to that red wasteland. We will, however, be regrouping on the moon while we plan to launch our revenge on the UE and take out the colonies."

"That's it?" Bali asked, knocking Eric's hand off of his shoulder. Eric could tell he wasn't comforted in the least as Bali went off on him. "That's your whole plan? Escape and take revenge with your merry men?"

"Oh? And you have a better idea?" Eric was now upset, he dare insult his battalion and his plan.

"I do, indeed. Once we escape this, we should still head to Mars Maximum," Bali said with a grin.

"Are you nuts?" exclaimed Cartwright, who was now equally as annoyed with Bali as Bali had been with him, "Why should we escape only to try and break back into the most secure prison humanity has?"

"Oh, please, that facility is not the most secure, just the most distant. It's the Alcatraz of humanity, and soon 10 Hygeia will be more so," Bali said, waving Eric's statement off.

Obviously to Eric, Bali knew more about these prisons than he did. Why should he care about prisons so far that he never planned on being anywhere near.

Eric kept listening to Bali, maybe there might be something to this that he could at least learn from. "They concentrate more on making it habitable because they don't expect anyone to get past the planetary defenses and the only way in and out of the facility is by transport.

"They made sure if you walked out in a space suit, you'd run out of air before you got to the nearest colony which just so happens to be Frontier Colony, practically a modern day utopia in space thanks to the Fallok family."

Eric was puzzled, he never really followed the colonies, just knew he wanted nothing to do with them. Obvious from his blank stare, Bali decided to give him a brief history lesson.

"Founders, leaders, industrialists and so much more, these guys are. They own that colony, and Earth just keeps giving them more and more money, people, and resources. They are softest there because they have virtually no crime, everyone is well-educated and employed. They have a nearly 0% unemployment rate, while people on mother Earth are suffering from 10-40% unemployment in the developed places.

"We should go to Mars, break into Mars Maximum, free the criminals there and convince them to join us. Then take over Frontier Colony and use them to take out the other two colonies. After that, we launch an attack on Luna, then Earth."

Eric was quite impressed. This was a nice plan, but there was on big problem with it. "Wow, Bali, that's very ambitious of you. But how can one battalion take out Mars' defenses, break into a maximum penitentiary, and then take over a colony whose numbers are over a quarter million? And then launch a military campaign against the home world? Wow." He couldn't help saying again, it was such a crazy plan. While his group did have its own unique way of recruiting since being cut off from the United Earth Defense Force, there was no way to get that many people to join a cause such as his.

"Al-Rashar Abdullah," Bali said with a smile.

"The Jihadist brainwasher?" Eric was amazed. He thought that guy was dead. But Bali just confirmed he's been at Mars Max for all these years.

"Yes, use the brainwasher to take over a colony, doesn't that make it easier?" Bali said with such excitement.

"Well, yeah, it does, actually. But once they know we are coming to Mars, surely they'll up their planetary guard and reinforce their capital."

"Yes they will, but we need to keep them divided. Use allies to make Luna think we are there. To make Earth think we are on Earth, and if Mars does find out, make them think we are going after their capital, which is Red Colony," Bali said nearly giddy with joy. Eric could tell he had been planning this for a while.

"Okay, I'm convinced; all we need now is to wait."

CHAPTER 4
The Great Escape

Near the Moon

Corporal Gian Eguia, pilot of Prison Transport 239-A6 was excited. This was going to be his second trip to Mars. More than that, his life was changing with this more than he had ever anticipated. This ship was going to be staying at Mars and then moving on to the 10 Hygeia prison. He volunteered to be the permanent pilot for this transport so that he could be constantly moving through space and seeing so much space had to offer.

He had just finished undocking the ship to leave the automated refueling station and was heading towards the moon to perform the orbital jump for the trip to Mars.

He had the two most ruthless men from Earth, and was going to take them to where they were going to spend the rest of their lives: mining to help humanity.

Because these two were so dangerous, he felt much more comfortable knowing there was an escort cruiser with two fighters escorting his transport to Mars. And he had his beta shift co-pilot Jessica Jensan on the ship, they had hit it off immediately on their last trip.

As Eguia was day dreaming of Jensan, he noticed a signal coming which pulled him back to the moment. Looking at where the signal was coming from, it was orbital control on Luna. He quickly signaled Gordon to the bridge and opened the channel.

"This is Prison Transport 239-A6, requesting clearance to enter Lunar Orbital Jump for destination Mars. Over."

"Prison Transport 239-A6, we must delay you momentarily; there was a satellite that crashed into some space debris and is in the current orbital course for your jump. It is being cleaned up and should be done within the hour. We apologize for the delay."

"Understood Control, but don't all satellites have proximity sensors to prevent that from happening?" Eguia asked, he was perplexed, as long as he'd been a pilot and studying piloting, he'd never heard of such an occurrence, though it did seem like a plausible one. Something didn't seem right about it.

"Yes, this one's malfunctioned. We are investigating, and I will contact you as soon as this is cleaned up."

* * *

"Understood, Prison Transport out."

Mian Wu closed the channel and looked up to her superior officer. "Major, they are sitting there waiting for us."

"Great job, Sergeant Wu. McAllen, how many ships are there?" Capperman asked, turning to his communications officer.

"Four ships, sir. The transport is in the center with a fighter on each side and an escort on the tail," replied McAllen.

"Signal the fleet to engage their escorts, prepare the grappler for the transport. Bridge to Farmer, ready your troops for boarding. Griffith, jam their communications. Whipple, bring us in for the attack," Major John Capperman said with a grin as he began his attack to a chorus of "Yes, sir." In a few minutes, they would have their commanding officer back and would begin planning for their next phase.

"Sir, we are in attack formation," Warrant Officer Falcon Whipple announced from the pilot's seat.

Capperman leaned forward in his seat and gave the command. Never taking his eyes off the screen he said, "You all know what to do. Begin the attack."

* * *

Major Gordon was in the captain's seat. "Report, Corporal."

"Sir, sensors just detected nine ships on an intercept course for us. They must have been on the other side of the moon. I'm reading heavy armaments and they're hot. I think this may be Hawkeye Battalion which would mean this is a trap." With growing concern, Major David Gordon took over the gunner's station and ordered all hands to battle stations.

Jensan was almost immediately on the bridge in the co-pilot's chair, reports of all other crewmen came in from their stations. The escort fighters turned from the transport to face the monstrous fleet. "Sir, I think we need to run, we can't fight nine heavily armed ships—they have us at 2-to-1 odds!"

"Control yourself, Corporal! We cannot allow Colonel Cartwright to escape custody! Have you contacted Orbital Control to request backup?"

"Yes sir, I've been trying since we saw the ships, all communications are being jammed. Can't contact the carrier or fighters, internal comms are the only thing unaffected." Gordon attempted to establish a lock onto the enemy vessels. He knew the clear sound of panic was coming out of his voice.

Knowing now that the debris message was faked, Gordon ordered Eguia to take the ship in for the jump to escape their pursuers. Gordon was shooting at them while Eguia and Jensan tried mercilessly to out maneuver them and get into the position for the jump. He wished he could see the progress of their escorts but he was too focused on saving their own tails to watch what must have been a slaughter.

"Damn," muttered Gordon just as the ship rocked. He had missed and they hadn't, Eguia saw that they took out the ship's last gun. Another shudder knocked out one of their maneuvering thrusters. They were definitely trying to disable no destroy. Another shudder hit, but this one felt different.

"What was that? It didn't sound like weapons fire," Eguia asked.

* * *

"Sir, enemy weapons are now disabled and grappling cables are attached," exclaimed Whipple.

"Good, send in the boarding party. I want on that ship the second we seal the air locks," Capperman said with his ever growing grin. A few minutes later, the boarding party announced it was departing for its mission.

* * *

Staff Sergeant Alice Farmer was ready to move in. Her troops had been preparing for this all week. In a few moments, she would be bringing her team onto the prison transport to get Colonel Cartwright and any other prisoners off of the transport and capture or kill anyone who got in their way. Major Capperman wanted them captured preferably. The Hawkeye Battalion needed more men and had been forced to recruit using more, extreme, methods than when they were officially part of the Earth military.

Suddenly a green light switched on above the airlock. That was the signal that the two ships were securely attached and her team was to begin their extraction. *"Boarding team Alpha, you are a go!"* sounded Major Capperman over the intercom. One of the men opened the hatch and the team entered.

Inside the ship there were few crew members. From what she had read in preparations for the mission, a normal crew complement for prison transports was seven men, two on duty at a time, two off duty at a time, and two asleep at a time, with one commanding officer. As this was a high profile prison trans-fer, the crew complement was doubled so there would be six guards for round the clock brig supervision. During an emergency situation, all thirteen crew members would be alert, armed, and ready to fight the boarding party.

As they entered the hall where the transport's hatch was located, four guards were standing ready to fire. Unfortunately, for them, her men were quicker. All four guards were down before they even knew what happened. The first soldier into the hall called out the all clear and the rest of the team headed onto the ship. They split into two directions, eight men towards the brig and five men with Farmer leading went towards the cockpit. Both teams cleared each room before heading on to the next one. Farmer expected Beta team to encounter five or six men and for her team to encounter the commanding officer and two or three other men.

When they approached the sealed cockpit door, Farmer hit the intercom next to the door.

"Attention crew of Prison Transport 239-A6, this is Staff Sergeant Alice Farmer of Hawkeye Battalion, we do not wish you any harm. We are here to free our commanding officer Colonel Eric Cartwright. We will kill if forced to, though we would like to offer you a chance to join us instead. You have two minutes to think it over, if you do not open the door and surrender in that time, we will come in and kill you all." She turned off the intercom and started her timer.

* * *

Eguia turned to his superior officer. "Sir, what are we going to do?" Complete horror crossed his face as he just heard this ultimatum by the leader of the boarding party. Surrender or die. He didn't know what to do. Major Gordon had a similar look on his face, as did Corporal Jensan.

"We must surrender. There is no way we can defeat Hawkeye Battalion, just the three of us. I don't want you to die. I'm opening the hatch and surren-dering," Major Gordon said.

Eguia could tell he was more concerned with himself than them, but he was more surprised that he would surrender without a fight.

Jensan spoke up with her beautiful voice. "Major, I don't mean to be out of place, but we were instructed to guard those prisoners with our lives. How can we surrender?"

Eguia nodded in agreement with her. Though he wasn't sure if it was more agreeing with her statement or just wanting to agree to whatever she said. He was terrified yes, but felt satisfied that whatever his fate would be, he'd be sharing it with her.

"Are you crazy, Jensan? I'm trying to save your lives. If we fight them we will die in vain. If we help them now, we may be able to stop them in the future."

Jensan and Eguia looked hopeful at that and then agreed to open the hatch and surrender.

Major Gordon walked up to the hatch and spoke into the intercom. "This is Major David Gordon, commanding officer for this transport. I am unsealing the hatch to surrender myself, my men, and our prisoners to you, Sergeant Farmer."

As soon as Gordon unsealed and opened the hatch, there was a blast and Major Gordon turned to his subordinates with shock on his face. It was the last thing the two saw on their CO before he collapsed from the smoking hole in his chest.

Eguia and Jensan looked at the dead man on the floor with such shock, they almost didn't notice as Farmer walked in. A tall and scary woman, she was still waving her rifle around but not actually aiming it at them.

"On behalf of the Hawkeye Battalion, I accept your surrender, Major," she said with a smirk as she looked down at her handy work. She then turned to the two shocked pilots and said with pure conviction in her voice, "He would have turned on us. This is the problem with captured CO's." Without taking her eyes off of them, Eguia watched helplessly as she began issuing orders to her people—orders that would change their lives forever. "Jackson, Valyir, take these two to the brig for transport to base. Holimer, take the helm and signal the ship that we have successfully captured the transport. Raul, come with me. Let's go welcome Colonel Cartwright to the life of a free man."

At that Farmer turned and headed out of the bridge, Jackson and Valyir came behind Eguia and Jensan and nudged them to start moving. He subtly went to hold Jensan's hand to comfort her during their walk to their own brig but she didn't show any sign that she wanted comfort. She seemed to show more courage than he was feeling. He was starting to wish he had her spirit. They made it down the corridor to the brig where they found all but two guards dead. These two had been captured but at the cost of three of Hawkeyes.

Farmer escorted them past the two guards and the other prisoners who had not yet been set free, finally stopping in front of the two cells at the end of the room. She turned to the two inhabited cells and released the locks allowing the men out. "Colonel Cartwright, it's good to see you again." The tall man with short blond hair and distinguishing features stepped up to Alice Farmer, and then pulled her close to him and gave her a long and passionate kiss.

After releasing her, he said, "Thank you, Alice, you did well. So sad though that these poor men had to die. But at least they died doing what they thought was right. Allow me to introduce my old friend. Former Prime Minister Bali Vritlianese." The older man turned to Farmer and took her hand.

"A pleasure my dear. Thank you for the rescue. I am in your debt."

Cartwright gave out a chuckle and took one of the radios from his men. "Cartwright to Major Capperman."

"Capperman here sir! I'm very pleased we have you safe and sound sir!"

"Yes, I'm happy to be freed as well. We are heading back over, and then let's get to base. We have a lot of planning to do."

"Yes, sir"

After the channel closed Cartwright turned to Eguia and Jensan. Gian was visibly shaking now. This man was staring at him grinning for what felt like eternity, then finally he spoke, addressing them.

"So, you two are the pilots of this beautiful ship." Jensan and he just stood there paralyzed with fear as Cartwright continued talking to them. "Well, since you volunteered to drive this vessel, I think it only right to let you continue to pilot it. Upon completing our Introductory course for becoming a Hawkeye of course. Until then, please enjoy the roomy accommodations you left me with."

Though he spoke so smooth and charismatic, Gian wasn't going to actually buy into it. Though he did silently get into Cartwright's cell as Jensan was escorted into Bali's. He couldn't believe how fast his trip of a lifetime turned into the barge of the dead.

CHAPTER 5
The Response

One week after the escape
Frontier Colony, Mars

Joe sat in the conference room at Geraldo Military Base, near the outskirts of Frontier Colony. Looking out the window through the protective dome and onto the air field, unprotected from the harsh Martian climate. He was nervously awaiting the arrival of the Frontier Colonies Civilian leaders. The Mayor was just another politician, they made him nervous from all the troubles he'd had with them back in Red Colony. The rest though, they made him excited.

Just then, a knock came on the door. As Joe turned the chair to the door, it opened to reveal an average height couple, both with brown hair and pale complexion. Joe immediately broke out of his nervousness and into a big smile. He always smiled when he saw his brother-in-law and best friend. Getting out his chair, he walked right over in long strides, arms wide open for a hug.

"Juliet, you look as radiant as ever." Joe beamed as he hugged her hello. Releasing her, he turned to Jacob, going in for a hug. "Jacob, I swear you are losing more hair every day. You know they have a cure for that right?" They all gave a big chuckle at that.

"You sure seem to be in a good mood today, especially given the occasion of this meeting," Jacob replied after the hug, though he held a comforting arm around Joe's shoulders.

Looking to his friend, it was always hard to not smile when being in Jacob's presence. The sheer positive energy that emanated from him, ever since childhood had amazed Joe. Looking to Jacob, still with his arm over Joe, Joe spoke the truth. "You know I can't stand Chuck. He makes me so nuts, as do all politicians. I really wish you had accepted that third term as mayor. It was yours for the taking, besides, Chuck does whatever you tell him anyways. He's too afraid to make the wrong decision so he just asks you."

Jacob frowned at that and replied, "Joe, you're much too hard on the man. He's trying his best, but being Mayor of so many people in such trying times, it's really hard. That's one of the reasons I stepped down, I needed more time with my family, and I love inventing things. Running a colony is cool and all, but making technology to better humanity, that's what brought my dad and I out here. That's what he died for. He spent his whole life trying to get us to this

22

place, this point, to help safeguard a future for our species. I can't turn my back on all of the opportunities he tried to open for me, and everything my children have done to further that."

Joe just smiled again at Jacob. This was the kind of person he was. Selfless to a flaw, Joe just wanted to keep him safe from others who didn't know him as well. Time after time, people from outside the colony never understand until they come to Frontier Colony, all the good Jacob and his family have done not just for the colony but to further the knowledge and better the lives of everyone from Mars to Earth.

"Are Jack and Richard coming by any chance? I haven't seen them in forever," Juliet said referring to her son and his best friend.

Joe smiled as the two entered the room just behind the couple. "As a matter of fact they are."

Having to bend over slightly, the lengthy Fallok, youngest of his siblings, caused his mother to jump as he hugged her from behind and kissed her cheek. "Hi, Mom, I've missed you, too."

Richard gave a hand shake to Jacob as he said, "Hello, sir, how are you these days?" Before Jacob could reply, Tyler LeJoines and his eldest son, Dustin walked in.

"Lieutenants, attention in front of a superior officer!" Tyler blared at the two young men while Dustin started chuckling.

"At ease, Lieutenants," Joe said with a smile, then continued a bit more seriously upon seeing Mayor Charles Graleen walking in next to Joe's other best friend, Robert Belington. "I think it's time everyone found their seats." After a few more hellos and muted pleasantries everyone quickly grabbed a seat. Joe walked back to his seat at the head of the table and hit a few commands on his tablet activating the holofeed at the center of the table. "I'm assuming you've all seen this transmission," he said as the report from Earth began to play.

"As the investigation continues, the initial reports are that the bodies and debris field found last week in the lunar orbit was that three fighters, two of which were the two escorts and nine bodies of the security crew stationed with the prisoner transport heading to Mars with Colonel Eric Cartwright and Prime Minister Bali Vritlianese confirming our suspicions that Hawkeye Battalion managed to get off of Earth to free their commanding officer and are in hiding somewhere in space.

"It is unclear where they are going, sightings and rumors have been coming in saying they are hiding out on Luna, or heading back Earth side, but it is

suspected that they could be heading out towards Mars to hide." A reporter finished as she turned towards her co-anchor to begin another story.

"On a related note, the Proto-type enhanced Solar Sail Engines stolen from NASA last month are now believed to have been taken by Hawkeye Battalion. If anyone sees any members of this group of renegades, they are to stay out of their way and inform their local military outlet. Here is a list of names and faces for all of Hawkeye Battalion."

Joe stopped the recording and looked at those gathered around the conference table. "You've all seen this earlier today." He began, "What you don't know is that a few days ago a satellite went down in orbit of Luna. It was hovering over a spot on the dark side. Here are the images it transmitted just before it was taken out." Joseph hit a few keys and brought the pictures of a military style facility barely visible on the moon.

"This was Lunar Base Six; it was built by Military Intelligence many years ago. We don't know when contact was lost with this base, but MI believes it was around the time of the trial of Cartwright."

"Excuse me, sir, but how does MI loose contact with a base and it takes them two weeks to realize something is off?" The chiseled, French native, head pilot for Frontier Colony interjected.

"That's the million credit question, Tyler. Unfortunately for that base, they were doing a drill that required radio silence for four days. MI had been trying to get back into contact with them after the drill but they couldn't, then this happened and they were told to investigate all leads about Hawkeye Battalion as their primary concern.

"It wasn't until this satellite." Joe clicked a few more buttons on his tablet and a series of images and videos played out on the holodisplay. "Sent this picture and then was shot down that we realized what had happened." Joe showed them the photo which showed Prison Transport 239-A6 sitting on the landing pad outside the base. Then a missile was fired from the base and the satellite was gone.

"My god," Juliet said as she grasped what all of that meant. "All of those people."

"Yes, the reason I'm showing all of this though is because a couple hours ago a fleet of military vessels went in to take out the base and capture anyone they could." Joe paused to a moment. This next part was the crucial axe. "The base was empty." Joe let that sit a moment to gage the reactions of the people around the table.

Jacob spoke up. "Do we know if they are heading here?"

Joe stood up at that and began pacing, a nervous tendency he had when dealing out hard to swallow news. "There was something else that we kept out of the news. It's about those proto-type Solar Sail engines that were stolen last month."

He took a deep breath before continuing. "The factory had only finished a few engines before the theft. After the Hawkeye's took what they could, they blew up the factory along with any engines they couldn't carry with them."

Everyone turned in shock at this, except Jacob, Tyler, and Jack who couldn't help but smirk. "What is it Jacob?" asked Mayor Graleen.

"Those proto-type engines are the last model," Jacob said with confidence.

"How do you know, dad?" Dustin said in confusion.

"I built them," he said with pride. "The first solar sail engines were built here."

As everyone digested all this new information, Joe sat back down to listen. He was unaware of the new model, only that Jack and Tyler were assisting Jacob with some tests. He listened as Jacob continued to unfold this particular secret project.

"Remember that big project I was all hush hush on a couple of months ago?"

"That was the solar sails? How come I didn't know?" Dustin exclaimed.

"It was a military project upgrade. Jack and Tyler were the test pilots for all the models. But we've been systematically upgrading all the trade ships with them as they dock. Any ship with leave gets the upgrade in exchange for some goods. All of the Mars military spacecraft were upgraded last year as well. We have two factories here in Frontier Colony and another two in Red Colony with one under construction in Kwying Ya Colony. We can send some to Earth. Aside from all that though, I can see why Cartwright would want to come here." Jacob said as he was obviously trying to bring the focus back onto the matter at hand.

"He knows about the Solar Sail project's origins?" Graleen asked.

Jacob sighed. He'd tried changing the subject. "I don't know, Chuck. As far as I know, it was above his pay grade to know. I doubt it would be hard to figure out," Joe answered for his friend, then he turned back to Jacob to continue. "But it still doesn't explain why he would come here."

"I didn't say that was why he would come here; I said I know why he would come here. But it's not good news," Jacob replied. Speaking in riddles like this, while entertaining for him, always annoyed Joe.

Not wanting any of these games, Chuck stood up staring across the table to Jacob, Joe watched Chuck raise his nervous voice to reiterate. "Him coming here of his own accord isn't good news Jacob! The question is why is he coming here!?"

"Chuck, have you ever read up on Colonel Eric Cartwright or his views?" Jacob asked calmly.

"Well, not really." Chuck said as he slowly sat back down, and calming his voice before continuing. "He has nothing to do with Mars, and being Mayor of Frontier Colony does keep me busy, as you well remember."

"Actually Chuck, he has a great deal to do with it, in views that is." Jacob was so calm and nonchalant talking to Chuck. Joe couldn't understand how he did it. "He is a strong believer that the colonies are leaches feeding off of the Earth more than when we were all stuck there.

"Eric Cartwright would like nothing more than to make Mars and Luna completely uninhabitable again." Jacob let that sit in a moment before continuing. "He views population control the opposite of us. When we see a population growing; we want to open a colony out in space to allow life to flourish. He views population growth as, there are too many people, and we need to kill some."

Everyone around the table grew wide eyed and there were some gasps as Jacob explained all of this. Suddenly some things were cleared up around the table and Richard Spoke up.

"You mean those massacres on Earth, those he called terrorists, they were…?"

"That's right Lieutenant; those areas didn't have any type of population control set up. There was famine in those areas and people were continuing to procreate. He couldn't stand this. He saw them as eco-terrorists, so he killed them to protect the rest of the planet. This man has some serious issues." Jacob said.

"How come he was allowed to Join the military and get so far through it?" came that deep British accent that Robert had brought with him decades earlier from his native England.

"He must have had some friends in the higher ranks that were able to hide him well. These views of his only came out when he was arrested," Joe answered. "While this has been enlightening for some of you though, the reason you are all here is that we need to come up with some defenses here. We also have something else of great value in orbit of Mars. The Destiny."

Everyone slowly nodded, Joe knew how much Jacob had invested in the UES (United Earth Ship) Destiny, humanities first massive space ship. So large it cannot enter a planetary atmosphere. Due to the proximity of technology and strong metals, as well as the general peaceful cohabitation of those on Mars, the Destiny was being constructed at a high orbit around Mars. Jacob had been on an inventing spree trying to come up with new technologies for that ship but a fast engine had still eluded him.

"Isn't that a long way off from being completed?" Chuck asked.

"Yes, actually, a couple years probably. But it still is important to keep what we have of it out of enemy hands," Jacob said. Then, turning to Robert, he said, "Rob, what's the status on Memory Alpha?"

The burly haired scientist straightened up in his chair now that he'd actually been called upon, "Well, it's nearly done. We need to upload all of our recent history and then put in the safe guards. As for defenses, that thing is tighter than Fort Knox. One way in, one way out. As you all know, it's 20 kilos underground and we have a shelter built down there in case people need to be evacuated from the surface along with rations to last four years.

"The only catch is that it can only house about 200 people comfortably. No way we could evac everyone to safety. Just mainly the politicians and other important people of the colony."

"We need to start building more bunkers then. And we need to secure the prison as well," started Jacob. "I suggest we have all construction workers on leave start working on Shelters all over the planet. We need to hide the civilians while Mars sees its first battle for survival. And we need to work fast. Start having all of our Solar Sail outfitted cargo ships currently at Earth or Luna, bring provisions as quickly as possible."

"But if Cartwright has a head start and Solar Sails, wouldn't he get here first?" Came Chuck's now accustomed nervous voice.

"No he won't. Tyler, show them your trajectories please." Jacob looked to the planet's top pilot who started uploading a map onto the holofeed.

"As you can see here," he began in his scratchy barely French accent. "In order for Cartwright to avoid being found by UE space force, he has to take a very long route to get here, even though his ship is faster, he may not know that only a few ships in the Earth fleet have Solar Sails."

"One moment, please," Chuck interrupted again. This was starting to annoy Joe. "You keep going on solar sail this solar sail that; how is a sail so important to all of this? We have orbital jumps to make trips shorter."

"Right, sorry," Jacob replied and explained. "Solar Sails take in a specific type of radiation that the sun sends out called Solar winds. These winds are absorbed by the solar sails causing propulsion. Once a ship pulls off its orbital jump, if it then launches its solar sails then they will actually be increasing in speed. It uses no fuel, so fuel is saved for jumps and thrusters, and it actually reduces the amount of time it takes to travel by another 20% or so upon the existing speed. This also works without an orbital jump, with just a cold start, you could launch from planet and initiate the solar sail right away and though you wouldn't be going as fast as the initial jump you'd get from the orbital jump, you would still achieve a relatively high velocity at some point during the trip depending on how strong the solar winds are.

"The new upgraded engine actually absorbs even more winds and uses the energy to help the thrusters and impulse engine as well as to help power internal systems. That is relatively new and only found here in Frontier colony at one of my factories. The proto-type is on my personal ship. Tyler and Jack just finished the tests on it last month and mass production started right away in the first factory. I hope that helps you Chuck." Jacob finished with a smile.

Chuck for his part was still trying to grasp it all. "Um, yeah, thank you Jacob for that…clarification. So you think Cartwright is going to take a long and windy path to get here?" Tyler took this chance to continue before he would get interrupted again.

"Yes, Mr. Mayor, you see. In order for Colonel Cartwright to leave Luna without detection, he would have had to initiate a cold start of the solar sail engine, in order to stay undetected on the shipping lanes, he would have had to veer far off course, Jacob and I think it'll take almost six months for Cartwright to get here."

"But," Jacob threw in, "we are going to go with the assumption that he could be here in as little as three months, so that is our goal to have all of our preparations completed before his fleet arrives."

Joe then decided to add some good news, "After sending all of this information to General Decker at Red Colony, he forwarded this to Earth and the CnC of the UESDF, Admiral Wong, has already sent a quarter of the fleet to Mars under General Decker's authority to secure the safety of Mars. They should be here in three months or less."

"Shouldn't we start sending people back to Earth as well?" asked Juliet.

"We can't," Joe said. "Due to population issues, people who've moved to Mars can go back to visit but can't move back unless the Earth's Population down sizes a bit. And let's face it. That'll only happen if Cartwright wins." This comment made everyone uncomfortable. "We may be able to send a few hundred back that can stay with relatives. I'd suggest women and children. We need anyone who can defend or build here. Mars is our home and we need to defend it from this monster."

* * *

As the meeting ended and everyone filed out, Jacob remained seated. Juliet turned to him when she noticed he hadn't moved and put her hand on his shoulder. He put his hand on hers and looked up to her and smiled.

"Give me a minute honey, I'll be right out." She smiled back and nodded, picking up her tablet from the table she then went outside to speak to Richard and Jack. Chuck and Tyler left the room discussing solar sails but Joe just kept looking at Jacob as he examined something on his tablet. Dustin and Rob noticed as well and the three stayed seated looking at Jacob.

Moments later Jacob turned up, looking at the three men before him and asked Dustin to shut the door.

Upon Dustin returning to his seat, Joe had to ask. "Penny for your thoughts?"

Looking again at all of them, Jacob hit a few commands and a three dimensional map of the colony appeared in the center of the table. Then they all noticed a spider web of tunnels spread throughout the underbelly of the colony. Jacob then began a new meeting.

"I'd like to add a couple secret things for us to build," Jacob started. "Rob, I'd like to put an extra emergency exit out of Memory Alpha leading to a secret liftoff hanger I've been building with Tyler." The map zoomed in on the link between the hidden hanger and Memory Alpha. "I'd also like to build a secret shelter leading from my house with a few ways to get into the colony."

Joe looked at Jacob in bewilderment, "But why Jacob? What's with all of the secrecy and hidden tunnels?"

"My house is in the center of the colony, it makes for a great web throughout the place for secret troop movements just in case. As well as for secret civilian escape routes. In case Cartwright gets into Memory Alpha, I want the inhabitants to have a way to escape off-world. Memory Alpha isn't just a project for us; it's a project for humanity. Our most important people will be held up there as well. They need a way to escape and a way to bring part of the Memory Alpha database with them."

"Interesting idea, Jacob," said Rob. "I like it."

"Okay," said Joe, "let's do it then, but I take it you don't want the others to know about it or you would have said something during the meeting?"

Feeling a bit apprehensive at that, Jacob had to tell them his thoughts. "You guys are my most trusted friends and colleagues, as well as the most important people in this colony when it comes to protecting it. We need to have these precautions set up. Chuck, for all his good intentions, is just a politician, and Cartwright will try and capture him if he can. Being Mayor of the most accomplished of the three colonies makes him a large target. We also can't hold him in hiding until we have to because his job needs to get done somehow.

"Juliet is worried enough without thinking these other things, and as good as Richard is, he is still just a subordinate. He can find out later. As for you Dustin, I'm worried as you're also in as big a target level position as Chuck is, but if we fail, I want you at Memory Alpha, ready to keep the fight going."

"Jacob, I don't mean to be blunt here, but you're Chief Engineer of this colony, you've invented most of the stuff that has made life out here manageable, and you are also the Lieutenant Mayor and one of the founding fathers of this colony. Your father was one of the most influential men in the colonization of this planet. Surely you are one of the biggest targets on this whole planet."

"I am well aware of that Joe, but this colony needs me where I am. That's where I'm staying. If I die." Jacob looked to Dustin and smiled. "I have three terrific children to take my place, and besides, for all of the opportunities this planet has given me and my family. I would jump to sacrifice myself to see those here live and grow. But don't get me wrong, I don't intend on dying, that's why I have my secret tunnels."

"Ok, then let's get this project going. Agreed?" Joe asked, and with mutual agreement they all rose and left the room.

CHAPTER 6
A Strong Defense

Five weeks after the escape

Within a month, the entire colony had signed on for the project of rein-
forcing the colony. There were some who felt that what the leaders
were doing was based on paranoia, that how could one battalion take over a
whole colony? Or, do we really have so little faith in our armed forces capacity
to stop an approaching vessel when we had more experience fighting in low or
0 G than the enemy? The answer to all this, "we know someone is coming this
time, if we stop them before they get planet side, great. But this won't be wasted
for the next time an attack happens and we don't know it's coming, we will be
able to protect, defend, and hide from the enemy." This single argument helped
persuade most of the naysayers.

More Moles, machines made to dig ten meter radius holes in the ground
were making the Job much more efficient and were being built as quickly as
possible, five could be built in a single week and fifteen new ones had already
been built and sent out digging holes first for elevator shafts to the shelters as
well as walking paths and tunnels to go between shelters, making them escap-
able and sustainable. The mapping of the underground caverns was reminiscent
of ant hills right down to the busy ants hustling all over in a type of organized
chaos. The schematics for the Mole had been sent to the factories in the other
colonies as well so that they could build shelters in case they fell under attack.

Though secretly, the Fallok family with a close circle of friends had begun
their own secret cluster of tunnels with an unaccounted Mole. These secret
tunnels had multiple doors and seals and dead ends in case the enemy found
their way inside, it led to all of the important parts of the colony such as the
factories, the space port, the Mayor's office, Memory Alpha, Geraldo Military
base, Joe and Jacob's houses.

Sitting at a work console in a deep bunker underneath the center of the
web of tunnels, nearly as deep as memory alpha Richard was getting to know
the newly created and highly classified Secondary Command Center. Though
this was still far from completion, it would have more than even the Primary
Command Center. He was monitoring security feeds from every tunnel and
shelter in the colony as well as the normal security feeds from around the colony,
and even had control of the atmospheric dome, air locks, you name it. Jacob,
Rob, and Joe thought of it for this place, they had to be thorough for it may

31

save their home one day. Richard was sitting in awe while also focusing on his secondary tasks for Joe; monitoring the work going on everywhere in the colony.

An alert popped up on his screen, it was an alarm telling him it was time to leave. He signed off and headed out of the bunker. He had a very important mission ahead of him.

A short time later, on the streets of the colony, in an outdoor restaurant, Richard Granit and Melissa Fallok were having lunch. The couple had been together for just over six years. Melissa's brother, Jack had brought Richard home during their first leave in the MDF.

Some say it was love at first site, though it did take a while to get through all of the barriers, two older brothers and the most famous parents on the planet. Not to mention six plus months of assignments away from the colony.

Richard had no actual family on Mars; he came as a child from Earth with his father. He had lost the rest of his family in an earthquake in Indonesia and his father brought the two of them to Mars to start a new life.

Sam Granit started as a construction worker on the colony and being a hard and smart worker, raised in the ranks up to a Forman in a fairly short amount of time. By this time, Richard had joined the Mars Defense Force. Unfortunately, while Richard was at the Academy, Sam suffered a severe heart attack; he died almost instantly and without warning, leaving Richard alone in this world, but for his one friend and roommate, Jack Fallok.

It had been a long journey coming to this place he was at in life. Looking into Melissa's eyes, Richard could not help but smile; they had just finished dessert, her favorite: Chocolate Soufflé. "How was your soufflé, Mel?"

She looked up and smiled in that mischievous child and very adorable way. "Mmmm, especially yummy today. I wonder what the occasion was." Richard and the staff of course knowing what the occasion was, the server stepped over to the table and set down two glasses of champagne. Richard thanked the server and then noticed the chocolate on Melissa's cheek, motioning to her, she immediately switched from happy to slightly embarrassed, and wiped her face.

Richard raised his glass and signaled for her to do the same. "Happy two year anniversary my love, and too many more."

He went to drink his glass after toasting her when she stopped him. "Um, Richard, dear, we've been dating for over five years and our anniversary was three months ago."

Richard smiled at that. "Yes, Mel, of course, but it's been two years since we moved in together."

At that she lit up. "Is that what all this is about?"

At that, he slid out of his chair and went down on one knee, he pulled a velvet box out of his pocket and looked up at her long brown hair and wide mesmerizing crystal eyes. They fell into a tearful shock as her face recognized the popular motions as Richard began.

"Melissa Rebecca Fallok, you are the greatest thing in my life. I have never in my life been happier than in these last two years living with you and I'd like to stay this happy for the rest of my life." Richard opened the black velvet box showing a ring with a big blinding red ruby. Never taking his eye off of her bright red and shocked face, that was so consumed with her beautiful smile.

He asked, "Will you marry me?"

She sat there with her huge smile and bright eyes, staring in shock at the ring. Richard felt like he had been sitting there for years just waiting for her reply, but it had only been seconds. Finally he could see movement in her face as the shock melted away and she began to form words.

"YES!" she said excitedly. "Definitely YES!" She confirmed as she went down to hug Richard nearly knocking him to the ground before he had a chance to stand. After the longest hug, they both came to their feet as he put the ring on her finger. They embraced each other again, even longer and harder until they heard the sound of applause.

They slowly let go of each other and turned around to see the whole restaurant staring at them. The server then stepped up from the crowd and with a big smile said, "Our guest chef would like to congratulate the two of you."

She stepped aside and Jacob Fallok stepped up in full chef attire. "Congratulations, I'm so happy to see this. Richard, I'm thrilled to have you as an official member of my family, welcome."

The three embraced and Melissa looked at her father, "I knew that soufflé tasted familiar, you two set this whole thing up?" Both men smiled and nodded, "I love you both so much!"

Richard was overjoyed at how well the whole plan worked. After setting it up with Jacob, he had his doubts it would work but Jacob had always looked after him like a son, and now he really would be a son to Jacob Fallok but more important, he would be the husband to the most amazing woman on Mars. He felt like his smile would never go away.

A week later, during the weekly family dinner with Jacob, Juliet, Dustin, Jack, Melissa, and Richard; Richard and Melissa rose to make an announcement.

They had been discussing this all week and decided to do it together, but Melissa would do the bulk of the talking, so Richard just held her hand for support.

"I know that Colonel Cartwright will be here anytime within the next two to five months, so Richard and I have decided to wed next month before any of this madness occurs, and because we are practically married on so many levels already, this is more a formality than anything." She had started talking fast as she began to panic with anxiety, but Richard kept her calm for it all with his gentle smile and comforting hand.

They looked out at the table to gauge reactions after she finished. Everyone at the table just sat there for a moment in shock. "Mel, sweetie, don't you want a nice wedding? Don't you want your family from Earth and Luna to come?" Juliet said in a slightly troubled voice.

At that Melissa frowned slightly as she began her response. "I do, Mom, I really do, but with trouble on its way, I want to marry Richard quickly so that we have that much longer together, should something happen."

Juliet started to cry at that thought and Jacob put his arm over her shoulder to comfort his wife gave his daughter a faint smile. "If that's how you feel, I will support it 100%, pick a date and that's what it'll be, we'll make it as big and safe a ceremony that we can throw. After all, it's not every day I can walk my baby girl down the aisle."

Melissa started to get teary eyed with happiness at her father's words, she released Richards hand and moved to him, he stood up and they hugged so tight. "Thank you, Daddy, I love you so much."

"I love you, too, Melissa."

CHAPTER 7

The Jasper

Out in space...

"Run! Run for the epod! They're breaking through the air lock!" The group ran as fast as they could toward the rear escape pods while the first officer locked each hatch behind them.

The first of the group approached the first pod, each one holding a max of four people, as it filled up, they sealed the hatch and ejected while the remaining three crew members headed to the second escape pod, as the third member was initiating the sealing sequence, the first member watched the other escape pod leaving the ship, escaping the attack, and then it came, a bright explosion encompassing the pod, it had been destroyed by the enemy.

"WAIT! Ian, don't seal the hatch! The others were just killed!"

Ian turned to the window and saw the debris. "My god, we won't leave here alive." Ian stepped out of the pod and went to an intercom. "If any of you are on board, we give up, we surrender, just please don't kill anyone else, what do you want?"

At those last words, Ian's legs fell out from under him and he slid down to the floor in tears. The other two were in the pod still, weeping with uncertainty, the terror of watching your friends and colleagues die was hard enough, but they didn't know who the enemy was or what they wanted with them, the cargo was basic mining and construction equipment from Earth to the asteroid field with a stopover at Mars.

Suddenly the was a thunderous sound coming from the other side of the locked door, the sound of heavy boots stomping in unison down the corridor, slowly getting closer. Every step was louder, it sounded like more than one person, but how many was it? They marched in unison and then, as it sounded like it was upon them, it stopped, then they heard the creaking sound of the door seal rotating, they were coming in.

Ian looked up at the door as it swung open, and saw a blur of dark bodies swarming into the room, as they surrounded him, their bodies blocked out the light, they made it darker as they reached down to him, pulled him up and began to drag him down the corridor. Behind him, he heard the crying of his fellow crewmates pulled out of the escape pod and dragged behind him. They were taken through the airlock onto another ship, a cleaner ship, they entered a bright room with clear walls, cells, the three were shoved into a cell barely big enough for two, as they looked around, they saw other cells equally over stuffed with people, hungry, crying, sleeping, all with one main thing in common, pure terror.

* * *

After what felt like days, a person in pure black clothing, black gloves, and a black helmet stepped into the room, removed his helmet and stared around at everyone; Ian caught his eye, and saw nothing, no remorse, no fear, just cold and darkness.

"Welcome to Hawkeye Battalion my friends, I am Colonel Eric Cartwright and you have all become my prisoners over the last four months as I make my way to Mars. Your ships have joined my forces as have your cargo. All I want now is your loyalties.

"Some of you have already given it to me, others have suffered, and then there are the new guys. You will be given standard rations once a week; per cell until you either swear loyalty to me, or die. You may do so either now, or at any time, hit the emergency button in your cell to do so. But I do warn you, if you swear yourself to me, and you betray me, I will first kill someone in your crew, then one of the other crews, and on your third strike, I will kill you. And none of those will be either quick, or painless. Do I make myself clear?"

At that moment, troops marched into the cell block, one person in front of each cell door, the doors opened and each person was asked, Join, die, or stay? In the end, out of forty-six prisoners, fifteen stayed, twenty joined, and eleven chose death.

As the first few of the last group were being tortured for any information they may have, the screams filled every corridor of the transport. A few of those eleven begged to change and join the battalion. That was everyone's first lesson, "once you make a choice, you stick to that choice." And their unfortunate choice stuck with every one of the survivors, awake and asleep.

Ian awoke with a jump a few days later, the screams wouldn't leave him, but that wasn't what awoke him this day, the alarm klaxon was blaring. He jumped out of his bunk, got dressed and stood in line at attention with the others for their inspection. The drill sergeant walked in and began her inspection of the new recruits. This was the sixteenth day. Each day after the first that someone failed inspection. They would be pushed out an air lock. Today would be different, at least they all hoped. The others who had decided to stay locked up had joined the day before after two people starved to death and were left to stink in their cells for a week.

Tomorrow everyone was being sent back to their ships for some engagement. As far as Ian had found out, there were ten captured ships as part of this flock, nine cargo ships and a passenger vessel. Everyone here was crew aboard those ships, no one had seen the passengers since their ship had been taken, and no one dared ask.

All Ian knew was this Cartwright guy was an escaped prisoner and his men were heading to Mars, it seemed that instead of getting there as quickly as possible, Cartwright was actually taking his time, he wanted people to stop expecting him to show so he could take them by surprise and while he took his time, he would capture every ship in his sites to use against the Mars Defense Forces. How this could be accomplished, Ian had no clue, it was nine cargo ships, a passenger transport, prison transport, a carrier which housed two interceptor shuttles, four fighter escorts, and a troop transport. But that couldn't be enough to go up against a planetary defense force. Ian was dead either way.

The next day, Ian boarded the Jasper, she didn't look the same, and she didn't feel the same. As he made his way towards the bridge, all he could hear was the screams of lost friends; all he could see was the blown pipes and dead bodies that he had passed just three weeks ago while running through to the escape pods, grabbing any survivors he could find. He made it to the front and saw the invaders of his world manning the consoles.

The man in the command chair stood up and turned to him. "Ah, Ian Slovski, welcome back to the Jasper. Your predecessor Captain Yugovich made a terrible mistake when we arrived; apparently he recognized us and attempted to send a distress signal to Mars. Luckily we managed to intercept the signal and Mars only lost contact for a few moments during our attack. Chock it up to faulty communications array and they were none the wiser. You aren't going to make that mistake if we let you pilot this beautiful vessel again, are you?"

Ian was shaking in his uniform, he'd hoped he wouldn't draw attention to himself, but it was too late for that. When his voice finally worked enough to make a sound, he weakly said, "Ye-yes, s-s-sir." The man stared at Ian for what felt like eternity, then, out of nowhere, he smiled. It was a scary, frightful smile, which then rolled into an even scarier laugh.

"That was pathetic, Mr. Slovski! You can do much better than that, especially if you'll be giving orders."

Ian was perplexed. "Giving orders, sir?"

At that the man stopped laughing and looked strange at Ian. "Oh, that's right, I haven't told you yet. Well, we're short on help, given the vast size of our fleet and lack of space training, we feel the best people to be running the ships are those who are trained in how to run and maintain them. Hence our recruitment program to which you joined, we are relying and trusting the crews of our newly acquired fleet to teach us as we head into battle. As the highest ranked officer aboard your ship when we acquired it, you are now the commanding officer. Though most of your crew will be my personnel so don't go thinking you can get away. We have special plans for you my boy. Now, do you have any questions before I depart?"

Ian thought it over a second and decided he may as well ask. "Um, sir, you know so much about me, but um, who are you?"

The entire crew began to chuckle at that, like he had just fallen for an inside joke. "I am Major John Capperman, Colonel Cartwright's second in command. You may address me as either Major or Major Capperman. And you will have a very important job for this mission, Captain Slovski."

"Me, sir? Why me?" Major Capperman stepped past Ian and beckoned him to follow. They made their way to the cargo hold where there was nothing but the two men.

"Do you know what your cargo is, Mr. Slovski?"

Ian, while not knowing where this was going, answered, "Construction and mining equipment bound for 10 Hygeia, we were to make a stopover at Mars though and we were secretly carrying some kind of cargo but I don't know anything about it. Only that it was going to Frontier Colony. The captain didn't inform me of the where or what with the package, but he did say that if it was opened by anyone other than its recipient, it would blow up the ship. I don't know if he was just saying that or if it was true he did love his jokes but none of us would dare to try."

Capperman chuckled at that remark. "Don't worry, Mr. Slovski; I'm not going to ask you to open it. In fact, you are going to deliver it, but with something else as well. You see, the item you were delivering was going to Geraldo Military Base, we are going to attach something to your package that will disrupt all communications within the base, and if all works out, it will spread to Borsovich Base and Ming Kim Base whereby allowing our forces a clean entry into Mars."

Ian was stunned. He was being sent on a suicide mission for a cause he had no part of, wanted no part of.

A woman then entered the cargo hold and stepped up to the two men. "Ah, Vekle. Just in time. Captain Ian Slovski, meet your new first officer and unofficial bodyguard, Sergeant Susan Vekle." Ian put his hand out to shake Vekle's hand, but she just stood there staring at him. "The Sergeant does have some tensing issues. She will have to work on it though if she plans on acting like a common crewmember and not military," Capperman said with a cold stare at the tall Russian blonde.

"Yes, Major, apologize," she said in a thick Russian accent. Capperman gave a light chuckle. Vekle, attempting to look more relaxed, continued, "Where is it you hail from, Captain?"

"Um, I was born and raised in Glazov," Ian said in his thick accent. He was starting to get less tense during this small talk with another Russian.

Capperman, now intrigued asked, "How did you go from a small town like Glazov to a cargo vessel?"

Ian, not seeing any way out of it, simply stated, "Eight years ago I was in St. Petersburg and I joined the United Earth Cargo Services and was assigned to the Jasper." In a slightly high-pitched, sarcastic voice, he echoed the words back then, "See space they said, help build the future of humanity."

Capperman smiled at that and asked, "And do you feel they kept their promises?"

Ian looked down at his feet. "If I said yes until the last few weeks, would I get in trouble?"

This actually made Vekle crack up and Capperman couldn't help laugh with her. After a moment, the Major composed himself once more and replied to the new and young captain. "Of course you won't get in trouble, how we can blame you for feeling that way? However, I do hope that in time that you will become a happy member of this battalion. After all you are so important to our plans, we couldn't do this without you, you know, and once phases one and two of your mission are completed, you'll have even more to do."

Ian looked up at that. "You mean this isn't a suicide mission?" Capperman looked to Vekle and back to Ian slightly perplexed.

"Suicide mission? Who said this was a suicide mission?" Capperman asked.

"You're sending me into the enemy's camp with the intention to commit an act of sabotage. How am I supposed to get out of that alive?" Capperman looked shocked.

"You didn't hear the whole plan? Oh of course not, we got side tracked. The package won't go off until you are taking off. Sergeant Vekle will initiate it from her station on board. That will also signal our attack. You will then head to Mars Maximum where our forces will be converging. While you are unloading your package at Geraldo, some of my people will be hijacking a new type of drill we recently learned about and once that's loaded and you are safely back aboard you will then meet up with us.

"Sergeant Vekle will be by your side at all times during this mission to ensure your safety. Understood?" Ian knew Vekle was there more to kill him if he failed or betrayed the battalion than to protect him. He was nobody, just on the wrong ship at the wrong time. He nodded his understanding Capperman adjourned the meeting. He turned to leave, halfway to the door he stopped and turned around, "One more thing, Vekle's identity will probably be known by the enemy so from now until your mission is over, her name is Tanya Oshlensolv. That was the next in line after you and your lover if I recall from the ships logs yes? Too bad she was in that malfunctioning escape pod." Referring to the escape pod that had been destroyed in front of Ian's eyes, "Have fun you two love birds." Capperman said on his way out, laughing.

CHAPTER 8
Finishing Touches

Five Months after the escape

Jacob and Joe were in Dr. Belington's lab for a meeting on the doctor's newest invention. "I give you gentlemen, the future in defensive weaponry for ground personnel in the colonies, the SRL-100," Robert Belington said in his light Wales accent.

The two men began looking it over and Joe spoke, "It just looks like a laser rifle, a cool laser rifle but yea, what's so special about it?"

At that, Robert began to beam. "This laser rifle is non-deadly, it only knocks you out for a few hours and it cannot harm inorganic matter, hence, it won't risk the containment domes in the colonies. It is completely safe for our use in fighting!"

Both men showed open mouth surprise at this, and Jacob lifted the rifle up and began examining it. "Wow, this isn't very heavy, in fact it may be lighter than current issue laser rifles." Jacob then aimed at a wall and fired causing both men to jump to the ground.

"Jacob! What the hell?!" Joe yelled.

Ignoring his friend, Jacob sat the rifle down and went to examine the wall. "No scorch marks, no heat, this is an amazing accomplishment Rob, how quickly do you think we can construct and disperse these around the colonies?"

Rob went to his notes. "With the materials and all, I'd say we might be able to produce 50 a day using your factory Jacob, but without your resources, it'd be maybe twenty a day."

"Okay, that's going to be a bit tough with everything else my factories are building, but I can put a halt on the solar sails for a while till we get these dispersed, we'll get a thousand in frontier Colony, then ship out 250 at a time to the others on a rotating schedule, I'll also send the schematics to my sister on Luna to get some made there, but first, have you had any bugs or defects with them?"

Rob searched his tablet for the right file. "Yes, it has a range of fifteen meters before it dissipates. You can get off fifty short bursts on the battery, which is rechargeable, or ten long bursts. It can over heat and blow up in your face if you hold down the trigger for more than two minutes on a full battery. And you can get an occasional gun that either fires backwards as in, at you instead of them, but that just happened when Johansson put the laser crystal in the wrong way. Or a gun that just doesn't fire. Crystals crack and what not."

Joe was looking at Rob with confusion but Jacob just stood there thinking. "How did Johansson put the gun together backwards and reverse the shot?" Joe asked.

"Yes and how can we duplicate it on the fly?" Jacob piped in with the air of an idea to his voice.

Joe looked then to Jacob and realization dawned on him. "Say, that's a great idea, if we can make it simple to reverse the shot, if a gun gets into enemy hands they'll knock themselves out for us."

Rob looked at the two men. "I'll have Johansson work on it right away and we'll send it with the schematics to your engineers."

Later, driving through the colony to Geraldo Military Base, Jacob was staring around at the sites. "Penny for your thoughts Jacob?"

Jacob kept staring for a moment, turned his head straight, and spoke softly. "Do you ever wonder if you're doing the right thing? What it's all about? We're making guns to fight, shelters to hide, five months of preparation, to go up against five hundredish people, and four or five ships. Don't you think we may be going a bit over board?"

Joe pulled to the side of the road, sat for a second, then looked to Jacob, "Over board? Listen to yourself Jacob. This guy isn't gonna back down, and he's not gonna slow down until he gets what he wants or all of his people and him are dead or incarcerated. Get a grip Jacob cause this was your idea, and as you said to others, eventually, even if we don't use all of this now, the future may require what we've built."

Jacob smiled, patted his friend on the back. "You're right of course, I started all this, I cannot allow myself to falter. Thank goodness that Rob came up with those non-lethal guns though."

Joe shook his head gloomily. "But Jacob, he just came up with that, Cartwright can show up any day, there's no guarantee that we'll have them distributed before he gets here." Joe began driving again, minutes later they arrived at the base, and then a bit after that arrived in the CnC.

Commander Lee came over to the two as soon as they stepped inside. "General, Jacob," she greeted, "reports are in from the Earth fleet, the upgrades to the ships are completed and they are being mixed into formations and rotations with our forces. We are getting all other information second hand from Colonel Elisabeth in Red Colony."

They headed over towards the strategy table. "Pull up the defense network, I want to see where everyone is," Joe told his people, moments later, the circular table projected a holographic display of Mars, its moons, and all vessels within three thousand kilometers of Mars with only a ten second delay. Ships taking off and landing all over the planet and fighters and tactical shuttles doing formations in space over the colonies. Jacob then noticed a couple weak spots; Joe noticed them as well and decided to do something about it.

"Commander, signal Brigadier General Elisabeth and Lieutenant General Jung and General Decker to Join us please, I'd like to go over our formations." The commander issued the request and moments later, three holograms appeared on specific spots around the table, Jacob and Joe stood in two similar spots and was projected to the other two bases.

The general spoke first, *"Yes, Joe what is it? I was pulled off from Earth for this."*

"Sorry, sir, but are you aware that our forces have two blind spots on their patrols?"

The general quickly changed from annoyance to concern. *"Show me."*

Jacob rotated the display. "As you can see General, your patrols are avoiding the polar caps, and that's our blind spot. We can't see it, and the patrols are avoiding it."

General Elisabeth piped in, *"Yes, the pilots were concerned about flying through the polar regions due to the blinding effect the magnetic field plays on the controls and sensors. You'd have to be crazy to fly there."*

Jacob was just shocked at this cowardice. "What the hell is wrong with you? Don't you see that we are dealing with a crazy man? Get some patrols in the polar region!" Jacob then began putting a projected flight course into the display while the brass was arguing. "Here is a projected course, if Cartwright manages to fly into the atmosphere through the polar region, he'll get the cover of the caps, followed by getting past all of your forces, then with his engines and the magnetic field to his advantage, he can make a sandstorm to hide him all the way to any of our colonies before we even know what happened."

The general took all of this in and turned to someone on his end. A moment later he came back on with the others. *"Jacob, how likely do you think Cartwright will do what you described here?"*

Jacob began inputting some variables and an equation and a minute later faced the others again. "If he sees no other way in but to fight or risk blind flying, my calculations show he'll try the stealth approach."

The general was eyeing the display, and then turned to his three generals. *"I see, well, do you have any suggestions for the patrols of these spots? We need our best pilots to be on the watch here."* While the others were going through their lists of pilots,

Joe spoke up, "Captain LeJoines, Lieutenant Fallok, and Lieutenant Granit are my three top pilots, sir."

General Jung then looked up from her PDA. *"Lieutenants Ming and Chan and Captain Slovina will join the patrol."*

General Elisabeth then received a message: *"Captain Jackson and Lieutenant Levitz. We'll divide the patrols into four teams, two teams per region running on twelve hour shifts."* Everyone nodded in agreement.

CHAPTER 9

The Invasion

Seven months after the escape...
Within Mars space,

"This is the cargo ship Jasper, request permission to land at Frontier Colony," the communications officer said to her counterpart on the surface.

"Permission granted Jasper you are clear to land at Fallok Spaceport, pad C. Flight instructions are being transmitted to you helm as we speak."

The helmsman nodded to the captain and communications officer. "Thank you, control, transmission received; see you on the ground."

After landing, it was relatively easy getting a truck and unloading the cargo, Vekle and Slovski were approaching Geraldo base. The drive from the spaceport to the base was quiet; Vekle drove and looked around, no doubt assessing the surroundings. Ian was looking around in awe, he had done this cargo route eight times now but he'd never actually been past the general vicinity of the major spaceport. He had no idea how beautiful this place really was until now, all the greenery, the parks, the open space, the kids playing, the farms. Wow, they actually have farms here, he thought to himself. They eased to a stop at the front gate security check. The 3 three MP began a search of the outside and underbelly of the truck while a 4th came to the window. "Name, Ship, Cargo, and Destination please?" He asked. Ian handed over his ID, Ship info, and the delivery ticket for the container and replied, "Captain Ian Slovski, United Earth Cargo Ship Jasper. I don't know the contents of my package, only that it is for Captain Joseph Ferguson's eyes only." The guard looked over the ship registry and noticed a different name for the captain. "This says Pavel Yugovich is the captain of the Jasper."

"Yes, he was... He and half of the bridge crew we killed when a piece of space debris punctured our bridge. I was the 4th in command and in my bunk when it happened. Unfortunately I was instantly promoted to Captain." The guard looked at Ian skeptical.

"When did this happen?"

"Around two months ago, we temporarily lost communications with Mars at the time." A guard came from the check point to his fellow guard and whispered something to him, the guard turned back to Ian and Susan. "Your story checks out and cargo is expected, please follow the guards in front of you to the loading dock." As he said this, 2 two guards in a golf cart pulled up in front of the truck, at the head guards signal, they began.

As they finished unloading the package and securing it in its position, Captain Ferguson approached with a woman and young man in uniform. The trio came to a halt in front of the couple, "Captain Slovski I presume?" Ian nodded. "I'm Captain Joseph Ferguson, I'm sorry about Pavel; he was a good friend of mine. Thank you so much for this. I bet you've been quite curious about what this may be." Ian couldn't help but nod his head in agreement. Captain Ferguson laughed at that, put in his authorization and the package opened.

At the site of the unveiled package, Ian lost his temper, "A desk? You had a desk shipped to you classified top secret for your eyes only?!" Shocked by Ian's outburst Ferguson turned defensive. "This is an Oak desk from the Civil War of the United States! It has been in my family all this time and my Uncle just died giving this to me in his will."

Ian was furious. "My Captain and crew died because of that desk! We could have went straight to Hygeia!" Ferguson looked down, "For that I am truly sorry, I had no idea that would happen. Though, in my own defense, I never issued those orders of classification, Pavel did to protect the package from prying eyes." Ferguson handed a tablet showing the transfer of funds from him to the ship. "Here you go; the funds are in your ship's account as well as a bonus, to help repair your ship." Ferguson turned and headed back to the way he had come. His attaché followed directly behind him, but the young man stood there a second looking at the desk. "Lt. Fallok, are you coming? We have a meeting we do not wish to be late for." The young boy turned quickly to join his CO. Ian and Susan went back to the truck and headed back to the spaceport.

For the last 30 minutes, Ian had been very quiet say for the tears running down his face, having enough of this; Susan pulled over and turned to Ian. "Are you okay Ian?"

Ian wiped his tears and turned to Susan. With pure hatred he said, "His desk killed my captain, my lover, and almost all my crew. I was captured, tortured, and blackmailed by your boss, but all of this was HIS FAULT! And I'm ready to help you take that snobby son of a bitch down!" Susan stared at Ian, and for the second time in two months, he saw her smile. But then she reached over and kissed him, long and hard. Ian did the only thing he could do under the circumstances, he kissed her back. She turned back to the wheel and resumed driving, but her attitude had changed, she was now happy instead of just following orders.

They arrived at the spaceport and decided to stop for a bite when team two requested more time for their objective. After enjoying the Martian grown food which they had to admit, was quite good; they made their way back to the landing pad, checked that it was fueled and inspected and met up with team 2 two inside. When they gave the ok, they initiated take off procedures and using thrusters, positioned into the Mash Driver, aka the Catapult. They shot into the air and, using thrusters to push thru the atmosphere entered Martian Orbit.

Ian turned to Vekle. "Hit the switch, let's bring them to their knees."

Vekle nodded and turned back to her console, pressed the series of buttons, and watched the communications channels die one by one, followed shortly by an armada of cargo, transport, and a few military vessels entering the region and attacking all military vessels in site.

* * *

On Frontier Colony, Captain Ferguson was having one of his weekly holomeetings with General Decker and the other two Captains leading the colonial forces. A few buildings over, underneath the still non disposed box that once enclosed a Civil War era Oak desk, a light begins to blink. Back at the meeting, the holograms begin to break apart, but not before all 3 three captains here the same report, all communications on the colony are breaking down due for no reason. Captain Joe Ferguson is now all alone around the meeting table.

He turned to his communications officer, "What the hell happened? We just lost General Decker!" His comms officer replied, "We've also lost all communications including our patrols!" Clarification dawned on Ferguson, "It's begun, sound the alarms, Cartwright is here. Get those comms back online!"

* * *

"Fire to disable guns and engines, we don't want to destroy those fighters unless we have to," Eric Cartwright said to his men.

"Sir," said his tactical officer, "picking up Earth fighters on patrol."

Eric was slightly shocked by this; he didn't expect fighters from Earth to have come and help the colonies, that's what his diversions were for. Of course he wouldn't let his surprise show. "I didn't want to take out Earth ships, but any Earth ship in Mars orbit should be considered traitors, and destroy them."

Cartwright looked at the tactical display noting the number of Earth ships was small, and the Martian fleet seemed only a quarter of what he had expected. The cargo ships for the most part were flying thru the battle en route to Mars Maximum with just a few noticing but unable to do much due to the battle. "Sir, we've just lost fighter Gamma! Cargo Ship Chekov is taking Gamma's position to protect our ship."

Cartwright, while sad at losing a fine pilot and ship, was happy the Chekov along with two other cargo ships carrying ships weaponry for the Chinese colony had successfully installed the guns to their ships, grossly surprising the enemy when their cargo ships were attacking them. Due to sheer surprise and the communications blackout, this day was looking to belong to Cartwright.

"Sir, the last of our cargo fleet has entered orbit and is heading down to Mars Max. The enemy's numbers are dwindling down and no reinforcements are coming. Orders?" His tactical officer announced from her station. Eric smiled, victory was his, and "All armed vessels are to protect our ships in space and above the target. Salvage anything you can out here, I'm going to my transport for the surface. Captain Louis the ship is yours." Eric said to his crew while standing from his chair and motioning to Janice Louis, his third in charge. He headed to a small pod and flew to the personnel transport where he met with his ground forces and Major Capperman. They would lead the charge.

* * *

Mars Maximum Security Prison

Dustin Fallok had just arrived for his monthly inspection of the facility on behalf of the Mayor of Frontier Colony and the Governor of Mars. As Frontier Colony was the closest colony to the prison, it fell under Frontier's jurisdiction for supplies, personnel, equipment, and in turn, the prison assisted the colony with bodies, Jobs, which all led to the combined benefit of more profit and growth for both the prison and the colony. On this inspection though, Dustin had been asked to come two days early due to a discovery made by the drilling team. They had just dug deeper than anyone else on Mars and discovered metals, assorted iron, nickel, gold, and a new metal that they couldn't identify. Dustin was here both as an official for the colony, a governor of the prison, and son of an engineer and scientist to oversee the first manned expedition to the new discovery.

In the control room, Dustin, the Warden, and assorted personnel and guards were watching the monitors from the EVA suits' head gear down in the caverns. The views were shocking; the assorted metals seemed so unnatural almost like they were there on purpose. Or perhaps, that was at one time the surface of Mars, but that would mean they were looking at a city billions of years old. Alarms then began blaring, taking everyone by surprise and forcing Dustin out of his train of thought.

"The prison's under attack," the warden stated as he changed the main monitor to the outside cameras.

Dustin looked over his should, and they saw cargo ships and a transport ship landing at the prison. "Where's the military? Why are cargo ships landing here?"

One of the other guards at a monitor screamed another then yelled over him, "Warden, the enemy has entered the prison!" He pushed that monitor's image to the main screen.

Dustin then blurted out, "Oh my god, it's Colonel Cartwright. He's here? He came all the way to Mars to invade the prison he was being sent to? We didn't see this coming. Warden, we have to get a signal to my father, he has to know we were wrong!"

The warden looked worried, his men scared, but he did a good job of hiding his fear from his men. "I'm sorry, Mr. Fallok, but we can't get a signal out, all communications are being jammed, including internal, and if Cartwright finds you here, it'll be nothing but bad. There is an emergency evac pod nearby that can get you to frontier colony, it was only made for two though and it needs two senior guards to access it."

Dustin looked at the man, totally shocked, he wasn't raised to run, but to help others. Helping others is why he got into politics, he couldn't run and sacrifice all these lives and this amazing new discovery could not be allowed to fall into enemy hands. "No, Warden, we must not leave until we have saved as many as we can. But most importantly, this new discovery cannot be allowed to fall into enemy hands. We must implode the hole."

One of the guards jumped out of his chair in fury. "But what of our people down there! They don't know what's going on!"

Dustin looked worried, and solemn as he stuck with his decision, "They may become the lucky ones in all of this. Send down whatever supplies and info we can, then seal this hole. The men will survive, but will have to find their own way out. And then clear the memory banks. The Hawkeyes must not be allowed to find any of this information."

The warden allowed for a moment of silence, then began barking out orders in compliance with Dustin's decision, for all they knew, they had just dealt a lethal blow to their men in that hole. A blow that may haunt them for what may be a not too long time, until their deaths.

* * *

Elsewhere on Mars Maximum

"Prepare for landing on Mars Max," Ian announced over the comms as his helmsman set course for the crowded landing. The ship slowed at approach and switched to vertical boosters for touch down between two other cargo ships. As this was outside, the cargo ships were docking to each other and walking through to the first ship for entry into the prison. As the crew of the Jasper, led by Ian and Susan strode into the prison they were greeted by none other than Colonel Eric Cartwright.

Cartwright looked at the incoming crew and grinned; he stepped up to Ian Slovski and Susan Vekle and patted them both on the shoulders. "Captain Slovski, Sergeant Vekle. You two did an outstanding Job!" The two nodded with a smirk and Cartwright continued, "Did you get the Mole as well? Outstanding!" he replied at their nods. "Come, both of you. I want you at my side for our victory. Capperman, please let the prime minister know, his kingdom is at our feet."

Capperman nodded and left the group and Cartwright led them towards the warden's office. Watching the fighting as it went on. Guards fighting a two front battle for their lives as the prisoners fight from behind and the invasion force battle from the front. They all knew the truth; there would be no victory for the forces of good this day. Fighting would be pointless, and so slowly, as they watched their friends and colleagues fall to the ground, the guards surrendered one at a time. Though no one would say where the warden was.

Elsewhere, in the control room overlooking the now covered drill site, the Warden watches as his men surrender on the monitors. "Dustin, you must leave! We must get out of here and warn Frontier Colony!" Dustin gave in, watching guards falling to the ground in some places, and surrendering in other places. Dustin slowly nodded and the two men headed to the door. "Sir! The enemy is breaking through to here!" The warden turned to his man with shock. "We all must get out of here, now!"

Just then, an explosion tore through a wall causing the room to collapse on Dustin, the warden, and half the men in the room.

* * *

Cartwright and his quartet stepped into the newly opened room, stepping over the shattered wall, they heard grunts and moans. As soldiers spread around the room looking for survivors and checking over equipment and giving reports to Capperman, Ian and Cartwright stepped over to a window overlooking a pile of dirt and a drill. Eric turned to Ian, "I think I know what those drill parts were for." Ian nodded in agreement.

"But from what I know of drills, this looks like a complete drill." Cartwright agreed.

"They didn't want whatever they dug up to be discovered by us." Capperman stepped over to them, "Colonel, these computers have been wiped clean. They obviously found something and were in a rush to hide it." The men heard a moan and looked over, two soldiers just freed a partially buried guard out of the rubble. "Bring him over here," Capperman ordered.

As the men dragged him over Cartwright flashed that arrogant smile and asked the guard, "What were you trying to hide from me?"

The guard spat at Cartwright's feet. Capperman backhanded the guard and Cartwright laughed.

"Okay, maybe we'll get back to that. Where's the warden? I heard he was in here. Has he left or was he buried?" The guard's eyes quickly shuffled down and to the left and back down, he didn't say anything. Unfortunately for him, Cartwright knew what that meant.

He turned to his soldiers. "The warden is buried under there, pull him out and anyone else. Ian and Vekle, go get the Mole and bring it here, let's see what the good warden wanted to hide from us."

The duo nodded and headed out to their ship, radioing in to get the Mole ready for deployment. With any luck, the soldier assigned to read the manual was ready to get it moving by now.

Capperman was overseeing the rescue assignment of pulling guards from the rubble.

"Sir!" one of his men said, signaling his attention. "We've found the warden and another man next to him. They are unconscious and need medical attention right away."

Capperman headed over to see. "Do we have a manifest yet, this may be a scientist who's part of this project," the soldier said. Capperman then bent down to the two men and scanned their faces to ID them and smiled. "Colonel! I have some good news for you."

CHAPTER 10
Mars's Max

As Ian and Susan were heading back to the Jasper to get the Mole, Ian asked, "So how are we supposed to get that thing from our ship to the inside of the colony when there is only one way in and there are four cargo ships and 9 nine airlocks between us and the entrance?"

Susan thought a moment and then replied, "You are too simple minded, we were at a dig site, we are driving a machine meant to dig tunnels, we will make our own way there from the ship obviously."

Ian though about that a moment as they approached the first airlock and cargo vessel and began making their way thru. All airlocks were being sealed and secured when not in use to protect against breaches, attacks, or escapes. "But what about the atmosphere? If we dig a tunnel from outside, inside, won't it bring the atmosphere into the prison and create a containment breach activating a lockdown?"

Susan stopped dead with shock, she turned toward Ian, "I take back what I said, that was a good observation, and you're right. What do you suggest then?"

Taking a moment to think, he began brainstorming aloud, "We can't just cave in the entrance once we're in, it wouldn't be secure, but we could install either a dome around the Mole entrance before we begin digging, or just create an airlock on the tunnel once we begin digging, but that could take a while, I'm not an engineer so I don't know."

Susan pulled out her radio and adjusted the frequency. "Vekle to Yaslov, come in." She tried a couple times. "если вы не пойдете сейчас, я скажу полковнику Картрайту, что вы заняты траханием пленника, чтобы помочь нам с его прямыми инструкциями."

They heard some loud noises on the other side along with some curses in response to Vekle's threat of telling the Colonel about his engineer disobeying an order to help them.

"I'm on my way, сука." Ian and Susan laughed as they continued on their way to the Jasper and its cargo hold with the Mole in it.

Once Yaslov had joined them in the cargo hold they began their planning, and arguing over the best way to do it. None of the other crewmembers around understood as the three spoke in Russian until Major Capperman entered. "What the hell is going on in here?"

Everyone stopped shouting and turned to the voice, Ian began, "Major, um, sir I apologize for our lag, we were working on the best way to carry out the Colonel's order."

"Really Captain? Because all of my reports show the three of you have been arguing for nearly two hours and in Russian. Well, what is it all about?" The three looked to each other and Ian and Susan pushed Eugene forward, looking back at the two who just sold him out, he faced his commanding officer and reported, "We are trying to figure out how to get the Mole to the dig site, sir. It won't fit thru the main entrance and if we dig a hole in, it will bring in the atmosphere, if we build an outer airlock or dome around the whole opening, it will be susceptible for attack."

Capperman was stunned. "Did you guys even look at the schematics of this prison since we got here?" They all looked too each other, then back to Capperman and slowly shook their heads no. "You're all idiots. When they added the dig site, they added a service entrance for large items near it. Just drive up to the airlock. You have one hour to get there or else." With that, he left the Jasper and headed to his meeting with his newest recruits and the former prisoners of this place.

Ian, Susan, Eugene, and Ian's assigned driver Raul Geoffrey pulled out of the Jasper's cargo hold in the four person accommodating Mole and headed toward the dig site, at the Mole's speeds, it would take them about 45 minutes to reach the service entrance, cutting it really close to the Major's deadline, they informed Colonel Cartwright's aid of the estimated timetable.

* * *

As Major Capperman entered the assembly hall, he took to the stage and sat beside Colonel Cartwright and Bali Vritlianese. Colonel Cartwright stood up and stepped to the podium once everyone was seated.

"Welcome to the first days of the New United Earth Force. You are all here because you either believe in our cause of ridding humanity of these colonies and solving overpopulation with an iron fist, or you just like killing others. Well today is our beginning. This war has started and Mars Maximum is our first victory upon the enemy's territory. For those of you who don't know me, I am Colonel Eric Cartwright of the Hawkeye Battalion, This—" He pointed to the former Prime Minister. "—is our President, Bali Vritlianese, and—" Turning to the other man on the stage, he continued. "—this is my right hand man, and you're superior in all things, Major John Capperman."

After the applause, Cartwright began his assignments for all of the new recruits and special assignments for the former prisoners. As he drew to his conclusion, he said, "We of course have one more thing to present to you all. Some of you may know the name Fallok."

There were mumbles in the crowd, the name Fallok was synonymous with the colonies and colonial tech.

"We have for your pleasures, Jacob Fallok's oldest son, Dustin Fallok."

Everyone in the audience jumped out of their seats in joy clapping, hooting, and dancing for a couple minutes until all settled down again.

"This present is to be Al-Rashar's first subject, all of you interested in learning the skills of our friend, please sign up for his classes in torture and brainwashing at the sign in tables outside the hall upon exiting. Thank you all and now I present President Bali Vritlianese."

Bali stood up and shook hands with Cartwright as the two men passed each other on the stage. The crowd had stood up to clap for both men as they swapped positions, Bali stood for a moment at the podium and stood waiting for the applause to come to an end, and he began, "My fellow Terrans, today we have made a large victory for our cause, with your help we will control this planet in no time. Once this planet is ours, its inhabitants will become our warriors in the ensuing war with Earth. But we will be victorious. We will defeat Mars, then Luna, and then my friends, Earth will fall to us. How do you say? They have more people, more ships, more resources yes. But we have one think that they pride themselves on yet will be their undoing. Rules of conduct and morality. Because of this we will crush them. They will not attack civilian targets, we will. And as it turns out, all colonies are civilian targets; hence this war is already won, by us."

This caused an ear splitting roar of cheers from everyone. Freedom, domination, and revenge were what they were just offered and just what they wanted after being imprisoned on this red rock.

Ian and his team arrived at the service airlock, requested entrance and after a few minutes of entry procedure were finally approaching the dig site. As they turned to the dig site they were met by Colonel Cartwright's aid, Lieutenant My Ya Jing, Ian disembarked from the Mole to receive his new orders from her. "Welcome back to the dig site, Captain."

By the way the lieutenant emphasized Captain, Ian knew this would be a rocky working relationship there was a lot of hatred radiating from her, to which Ian could not tell why. In truth, she hated all of these new captains in the battalion. My Ya Jing had been a soldier in the UEF for 15 years and hadn't accomplished nearly as much as she had wanted to. Merely a lieutenant and an aid to a commanding officer instead of being a commanding officer.

Then over the six months trip from Earth all of these new members to the battalion were forced into it against their will, could turn at any time and yet are made Captains and XOs and Chief Engineers merely at the whims of Colonel Cartwright.

My Ya continued her address to the young captain upon his thanking her for the welcome, "The Colonel and Major are currently busy but here are your orders, since the drill was sabotaged by Fallok and his people, we need your team to take the Mole and re-dig this hole. We need to know what they were hiding and why it's so important to them. From what I'm told you currently have Susan Vekle, protection, Eugene Yaslov, engineer; and Raul Geoffrey driver and engineer, correct?"

Ian nodded and gave a, "Yes, ma'am."

My Ya continued, "Yes, we will be swapping out Yaslov as you have two engineers, and giving you Doctor Elisabeth Groeneg, she is a doctor of archeology."

Ian went slack jaw at this. "We have a doctor of archeology among our ranks?"

My Ya raised her eyes at him. "Captain, control your emotions please. Yes we do, how is need to know info that you don't need to know, as well as how we know she will be loyal and open to us."

Ian slowly nodded and the lieutenant turned and headed inside the dig site with a nod for Ian and the Mole to follow her.

Once inside, Ian radioed for Yaslov to come out and he met Dr. Groeneg. Jing gave him his map and other encoded information and the team set off. Ian reflected on this, he had now gone from pilot and fourth in command of a cargo vessel to captain of that vessel, to espionage and now captain of an excavation team.

He was actually starting to enjoy his new job that kept rewarding him with responsibilities and promotions, as much as he feared these people, since joining them he had slowly been understanding what they were fighting for, seeing how that Captain at Frontier Colony had just brushed off the death of a friend and most of the crew of a civilian ship en route on a mission for him.

The arrogance of these colonists, the high levels of overpopulation on Earth, the fact that the world had to adopt the law of one child per family 35 years ago because the planet could no longer sustain 12 billion humans and that colonists such as the Fallok family could have three kids with no worries about the resources they are taking from others. The colonies had to fail and humanity needed to be cut down 3/4ths to preserve the home world they all claim to care for.

This was now his time to shine, he shook out of his revelry and climbed back into the Mole. "Okay, team, let's see what's down there."

With that quick line of inspiration and order, Raul switched the motor on and into drive and the Mole tilted towards the exposed Martian dirt and began its long dig.

CHAPTER 11

12 hours ago

"Cartwright is here? On Mars?" Captain Ferguson nodded. "And how did he get thru our defenses?"

Joseph Ferguson was torn, embarrassed and stunned by the report he had read before this meeting with his longtime friend and associate, Jacob Fallok. "It was my fault." Jacob fell silent at this, stunned and speechless.

Joe continued, "The cargo ship Jasper arrived with a family heirloom from home, hidden on it was a viral transmitter that sent a computer virus into our communications array. After checking over the tapes of the Jasper crew, we discovered that most of the crew were Hawkeyes, the ship had been taken over, as well as eight other cargo vessels and a civilian transport. That's why they took their sweet time coming here; they were amassing a force to get here. I was in my daily meeting with the other colonies when they struck their virus, it spread to them because of us. Also we discovered that they stole a Mole while they were here."

Jacob had sat down during this confession, he was faltering. "Where are they?" he asked.

Joe came around his desk to get closer to his friend. "Mars Maximum."

Jacob looked up, they both knew Dustin was there overseeing a new discovery. "My son may be dead or captured because of your oversight." Jacob stood up; he turned and left the office, leaving that in the air. He went to his car and headed to his wife's lab, he had to tell her and the kids about Dustin, and that the battle has begun.

A short while later, after he'd called Jack, Richard, and Melissa and told them to meet him at Juliet's lab; he informed them of the situation and Dustin's currently unknown status. Jack stood up, "I remember that, I was with Captain Ferguson when he received his desk."

Jacob looked shocked, "Desk? That was his 'Family Heirloom'?"

Jack nodded and continued his recount, "You aren't the only one who was shocked, dad. The cargo ship captain was this guy a little younger than Mel, he said his Captain and most of the crew died on the way here and that the only reason they even came to Mars was to deliver that package that the previous captain had deemed classified. The rest of their mission was for 10 Hygeia and that none of this would have happened if it weren't for that desk."

Juliet had to ask, "What's so special about this desk that he had it delivered from Earth?"

Jack replied, "It's an oak desk from the American Civil War. His grandfather died and sent it to Captain Ferguson in his will. The desk was handmade by his ancestor who was a captain for the Union army."

At that Jacob had to concede, "Well, that's definitely an heirloom, wow. But what happened with the cargo ship captain?"

Jack continued, "He was pissed, he nearly went all out on Captain Ferguson, to which the Captain said, he was sorry for the loss as the original Captain of the Jasper had been a friend of his and he gave them a bonus over the pay, as an apology. I could tell looking at this guy that more money wasn't what he wanted. When he arrived he was scared about something, he was shaking slightly and really nervous, when he left though, he was angry and shocked and I think hurt by Captain Ferguson."

Jacob thought it over a second. "You said he was with a woman, yes?"

Jack nodded.

"What was she like?"

Jack thought for a minute. "She seemed in top shape, strong, great body, but really tense and I couldn't really read anything off of her, she never spoke."

Juliet was watching Jacob's reactions, as was everyone.

Melissa spoke in then, "Daddy, what are you thinking?"

Jacob turned to her, and after a moment, began, "She was a Hawkeye. I'm certain of it. They killed most of the crew on these ships and forced the survivors to join them. This captain was probably the highest ranked survivor from the Jasper so of course he wouldn't go anywhere without a Hawkeye watching him closely."

Juliet had a thought, interrupting Jacob, she said, "Jack, how upset was this man?" Thinking a second, "Captain Ferguson may have made an enemy with him."

"Why?"

Jacob was seeing it too. Juliet replied, "We could have had an ally in the ranks of Cartwright's army, and Joe just thru it all away and gave us another enemy."

"I'll set up a meeting with Joe later tonight; we need to have a serious discussion on professionalism to others as well as a plan to take care of this mess." Juliet seemed seething at this, "That's it? That's all you have to say?" Taken aback, Jacob asked what she meant, "Your best friend, and the head of this colony's defenses screws up, big time, and now our eldest son is likely dead or captured, and you're going to talk to him about his attitude towards others?"

"It's the only thing I can do; Joe is as much a part of this colony's protection plan as the rest of us are. If not more because of his position, a position to which we have no influence or control over." With no alternative but to concede, Jacob headed out, he had some planning to do, and videos from the prison attack to view in his control room. Jack and Richard trailed along to assist.

As he drove to the secret bunker at their house he spoke to the boys about what to look for, "Jack, examine the logs of the space battle and the surroundings of Mars Max, I want to know what happened and then how we can take back the prison and deal the Hawkeyes a devastating blow if we can. Rich, you need to go through the internal videos from the mars max attack and see what happened as well as what has happened to Dustin. Any questions?"

Richard asked, "Sir, the Hawkeyes have been jamming sensors and shooting satellites around Mars Max since the attack, we don't have any of that information to peruse."

Jacob grinned at that. "No you don't, but the Hawkeyes do. Do you honestly think a group of Earth commandos could prevent Mars' top engineer from hacking through their jammers and into their communications system without them knowing it?" Richard softened up a bit at that, well when you put it that way, I guess you're right."

Jacob laughed. "Yep, that's why I sent an encrypted message to Rob and TR to meet me at the control center, this is gonna be a tough job."

Both boys were shocked. "But you just said—"

"I said Mars' top engineer, that's not just me, I'm an inventor yes, but Rob is an artist with firewalls and encryption and TR is the top hacker on Mars, so of course I'd keep both of them close by to help me with just this type of operation." The boys were shocked and surprised after always thinking of Jacob as the smartest man on Mars though at the same time who doesn't want to think of their father as the smartest or best man around.

As the three men entered the secret bunker, they were met by Rob and TR already hard at work in the enemy computers. TR would breach and Rob would place a protective barrier behind him both hiding their presence and keeping a path in the systems for the team to repeatedly enter through.

Jacob approached the two hard working geniuses as cautiously as he could so as to not startle them, until his funnier side just couldn't stand it and he yelled "HI!" causing Rob to jump and TR to laugh.

"What the hell Jacob! You know we're working!" Rob exclaimed, causing TR to laugh even more,

"Rob, you didn't hear those footfalls coming from across the room or the elevator ding when it opened?"

Rob stopped his outburst and just looked down. "No, I didn't."

Jacob, not wanting to kill a good thing, decided it was time to focus. "Okay, fellas, we're all here now, we'll keep hacking through, Richard is going to be searching thru the internals and Jack will examine externals, boys take you console to the left, I'll relay your info to your screens." With that all five began busing themselves with their terminals.

As Jack watched the space battle commence he felt a pang of guilt watching his friends and allies being blown to their deaths thru the eyes of the enemy, until he noticed something, "Dad, they seem to be only disabling our ships, it looks like their objective is to disable and capture instead of attack and destroy."

As he said this he watched the Earth Force fighters enter the engagement and the Hawkeyes showing no mercy to them. By this time Jacob had come and was looking over Jack's shoulder at the monitor.

"Cartwright sees Earth ships protecting Martian interests and considers them traitors to Earth. Traitors should be killed on site, military directive for years."

Jack hearing this only seemed more confused so Jacob decided to clarify, "Cartwright believes he's looking out for humanity, Earth is still his ally in his mind, until he is ready to take them out."

Jack seemed to get it more and turned to get back to viewing the battle. A few minutes later Richard spoke up, "Jacob, I see what Dustin was doing."

Jacob rushed over and so did Jack to which Jacob gave him a menacing stare he used to get as a kid to go back to what he was doing instead of rushing to a distraction. Jacob stared over Richard's shoulder at the monitor as they watched Dustin going over plans and talking with researchers at a dig site in the prison.

Suddenly everyone went from relaxed to alert and Dustin and the warden were looking over shoulders and then discussing something and Dustin began giving orders. A man stood up from his seat to object to something but Dustin and the warden held their ground. A moment later Dustin initiated a cave-in at the hole, moments later the wall beside Dustin collapsed as well as the video feed.

Jacob spoke then, "I think Dustin is alive, and now we know he covered the dig site to protect it, though that'll only be a temporary measure. We need to find out what was there. Good work Richard, keep searching." Richard nodded and continued perusing through.

About half an hour later Jack called Jacob over again, "Dad, it looks like one of your Moles coming out of the Jasper. It's heading to the dig site service entrance I think."

"Jacob, there is a base wide transmission going out, I'm hacking it and putting it on speakers," TR announced and they all sat listening to the speech by Cartwright and Bali. When Cartwright mentioned Dustin becoming the first of Al-Rashar's victims, Jack stood erect nearly ready to bash the first person to cross him, and Jacob sat down in shock and grief. Richard and the others finished listening then turned to Jacob.

"We need to do something Jacob, time is running out if it hasn't already. We're lucky that this is a live transmission so we have till morning to rescue Dustin." Richard said, very not reassuringly.

Jack turned to his dad, "So what's the plan?"

All eyes went to Jacob, at that moment Joe walked into the room.

"Good you're all here, we need to get some Intel from MM we just got communications back up and satellites are en route."

Jacob was slightly shocked by this. "Um, Joe we hacked into the enemy systems and got full footage of everything."

Joe's smile, jaw, and broad shoulders all took a slouch as his surprise was absorbed, though this did not last long as he then looked to Richard and Jack then to Jacob and became angry. "You two may be part of the Fallok family, but as long as you wear those uniforms, you must answer to me. We've had a crisis here and you needed to be at your posts! And you knew that Jacob. And hacking into enemy systems without notifying me? I run the military operations of this colony, gaining Intel is my Job and I should be in the loop."

Jacob became so angry at this outburst while the two young men hung their heads and Rob and TR just watched unsure what to do. Jacob retorted, "Don't you dare start on me Joe. We will talk but first, we have two objectives to achieve."

Joe, while still vented, eased a bit and asked, "We do?"

Jacob nodded and began, "Dustin covered the whole the was beign researched, the Hawkeyes figured out there is something under there and are probably already using the Mole they stole to drill down the hole. We need to send two Moles to intercept them or at least to prevent them from reporting their findings to the surface, but we also need to find out what is so important down there.

"Objective 2, Dustin has been captured and will be interrogated by Al-Rashar tomorrow morning. We need to rescue him before he can divulge any information on our strategies to them. Juliet needs to be part of the team to go to the dig site, her specialties are imperative for finding out what's down there. Joe we should deploy missiles to take out their ships on the ground and coordinate the rest of our forces to take down their ships in orbit."

Joe just stood there a moment, and then nodded. "Uh, yea, of course, great plan. I'll go back to base right away and begin coordinating our joint attacks. But bear in mind, I will have to give the extraction team orders to kill Dustin if they can't rescue him. He's too valuable alive to them. And we'll need to use a Mole for that mission, only way since we can't very well bomb the installation."

Jacob slowly nodded, knowing that he was signing his own son's death certificate with that son's godfather, and another godfather and two sons watching. Whatever happens to Dustin now will haunt Jacob for the rest of his life.

CHAPTER 12

Joe was heading back to base with Jack and Richard in toe. The two men were filling him in on the Intel and Jacob, Rob, and TR were continuing their surveillance. As soon as they entered the base, Joe proceeded to give his report to his counter parts in the other colonies and his CO. Upon their agreement, Joe was taking command of the black op into Mars Maximum while Captain Elisabeth oversaw the space assault and Captain Jung, the bombings.

Jacob had begged Joe not to mention the dig as it would present a dispute over who should claim it. Since it was under Mars Maximum which came to the purview of Frontier Colony, they both agreed it needed to stay an internal matter, Jacob was overseeing all ops from his CC and Juliet was going to take two teams down to the site, one an intercept team to stop whoever Cartwright sent and team two would be an ensemble of scientists, with Richard joining as an escort and driver.

Joe had ordered Jack and Tyler to standby positions in case they needed to help with the air or space assaults. Joe felt the Black op would have to be free of any Falloks, due to the emotional situation of it being one of them they were planning to rescue. This was one mission, Joe felt he had to go on, so he would be leaving Commander Lee in charge while he leads the op into enemy territory.

He assembled his top three people to come with him, Lieutenant Commander Marshals, marksman; Lieutenant Commander Fostrell, hand to hand combat; and Lieutenant Jeremy, combat technician. He then assigned Commander Korskiev to lead the interception mission with Lieutenants Harvet, Romo, and Katrolla. Jacob had just sent him a text saying Juliet was taking her assistant Kevin Daniels and Dr. Helga Johannesburg.

There were a few complications with the missions as the Moles can only travel at 24 kph which would make the trek around 24 hours. They had 14 hours though so a remote transport shuttle was taking the three teams halfway and then landing and creating cover to allow the Moles to still sneak into the enemy's new territory.

Once they landed at their departure point, all parties broke and went to their Moles and headed out. Time was of the essence. As Joe got into his Mole, Lieutenant Miranda Jeremy was manning the helm, so he took a seat beside her and allowed her to proceed. During this long trip the team took turns driving, sleeping, and Joe spent a lot of time thinking.

Joseph had felt terrible since finding out that he fell right for Cartwright's trap, and even more so for how he treated that young man. He had run it through his head countless times wondering each time, why he had been so rude to the boy. He had been in such a rush when the delivery came to get to a briefing that he rushed through without thinking. He couldn't afford to be so negligent on this or any other mission or choice and especially not to other people.

Joseph had been born and raised on Luna 47 years ago, moving to Mars when he was 17 near the beginning of the colonization of Mars. He lived in Red Colony for six years, then left to help build Frontier Colony. He had come from a wealthy family and had a sister who still lived on Luna. She was married to Jacob's sister, Jasmine Fallok, and was a robotics engineer.

Growing up and living in colonies was a tight existence but at the same time, with Earth's population nearing a standstill and Luna and the space stations being mainly research, mining, and military facilities, Mars was encouraged to grow both in population and industry. Martians today had it easier than just about everyone on Earth. Luna and life was only getting better as Frontier's growth brought growth planet wide. Truth be told, a class structure even occurred, though mostly by accident. The Kwying Ya Colony had the strictest, determined and disciplined citizens.

Red Colony was a political and governmental mesh from Europe, Russia, and the Americas with bright, greedy minds mixed into bureaucratic non-sense. And finally Frontier Colony, a corporately owned colony run by a Board of Directors posted by each company and a Citizen-elected Mayor to head the Board and make everyday decisions. Here, education is more open and life is more scientific

"Captain, your turn. Captain Ferguson, please wake up." Joe felt a shaking and opened his eyes, he'd fallen asleep. Lieutenant Jeremy was staring at him.

"Sir, it's 0330 hours, your shift," she said.

Joe caught himself, agreed and stood to switch positions with her followed by Fostrell switching with Marshals in the navigation chair. Thanks to cutting the time in half, four six-hour shifts were broken down to three four hour shifts and they were making good time.

* * *

Vladimir Korskiev was intrigued by his newest mission. He was a little jealous of his commanding officer, Captain Ferguson, for taking his best three men for a black op into enemy territory to rescue a VIP hostage. But to go and encounter the enemy in an unknown landscape, unaware of what was there while at the same time protecting a group of scientists and what they believe to be a great discovery.

Vladimir felt ashamed with himself for being jealous of one assignment over another especially when both were equally hazardous and critical. He was a born leader, born in Russia; Vladimir came from a military family and joined the UEF as soon as he came of age. Fifteen years ago he volunteered to transfer to the Mars Defense Force and was assigned to Frontier Colony following a five year stint in Red Colony.

As part of his tour of duty, he should have been transferred to Kwying Ya five years ago, but Captain Ferguson and promoted him and granted him a permanent position in Frontier. Turning his attention to Romo and Katrolla in the front, he listened for a moment to what the two men were discussing.

Romo had recently become a father and was asking Katrolla questions as the older man was already a father of 2. As a career officer constantly on the move, Vladimir hadn't settled down with anyone yet, sure he had a girlfriend here and there, currently he was in-between relationships.

Vladimir spoke up interrupting the two. "Romo, update please."

Romo sat up slightly and went over his readings. "Well, sir, we are digging 12 kilometers deep at a 38 degree angle to reach the estimated bottom of the drill site which was 300 kilometers away from our departure point."

Vladimir rolled his eyes at this, he knew all of that already he just wanted an update. Romo sensed this and quickly got to the point. "We are nearing half way there sir, and we are five kilometers deep and have gone 144 kilometers so far."

"Thank you, Romo, do you two need to switch with us? How are you holding up?"

The two looked to each other and smiled, Katrolla replied, "We're fine, sir, enjoying our talk on kids."

Vladimir gave a chuckle and sat back and pulled out his Tablet to go over reports and make some notes in his log. "Okay, men, carry on."

* * *

Richard looked at his display; they had traveled 143 kilometers and just about five kilometers deep. Staying a steady kilometer behind Team 1 by following them instead of creating a second tunnel, it increased their chances of arriving with minimal problems, in case a drill broke, Team 2 would take lead and what not. Focusing on his mission was the only way Richard could keep his mind off of Mel and the pain she and the rest of the Falloks were going thru once they found out about Dustin.

When Juliet had insisted on going on this mission, Richard volunteered as well and promised Mel he would look after her mother, his mother now too. Juliet woke from her nap just then and tapped on Kevin's shoulder to relieve him from navigation.

After she settled in she turned to Richard. "How are you doing, Rich?"

Richard was caught off guard with the question. "Um, shouldn't I be asking you that Juliet?"

She shook her head. "No, I'm going to be okay, I know Joe will get Dustin home safe. But I was asking you because you haven't switched with anyone, aren't you tired?"

While he was a bit tired, he was charged with protecting Team 2, this was his first solo mission and he wanted to do well for himself, the team, and because this was the first time he had ever worked with Juliet let alone spend so much time alone with his mother-in-law.

"I'm fine; this is all part of my training," he said. As she settled in a bit, he asked, slightly nervous, "Do you know anything about this discovery?" Richard was curious but also wanted to change the subject.

Juliet saw thru his plan in a heartbeat, but humored him.

"I'm not quite sure but from the reports we got before we sent Dustin and that clip that Jacob showed me of the dig site, they discovered some new type of metal or ore, though from what the excavation team reported and Dustin agreed on, is that they think it's an unnatural material mixture in unnatural formations."

Kevin was listening and Helga had awoken as well and heard, then she blurted out, "You mean Dustin thought there was a city down there?"

Juliet nodded and Richard and Kevin's jaws dropped. "By the strength of the metal, and that some formations are still intact, I'd gather that it was a pretty advanced civilization. And by the depth of this city, if it was ever on the planet's surface, it predates Earth."

Richard thought there was some mistake in his understanding. "By Earth, you mean mankind? Dinosaurs?" he said, Juliet shook her head though.

"No, I mean the formation of our planet. Scientists around the turn of the millennium, late 1990s early 2000s, surmised that Mars was here long before Earth. Some even believed Mars was a little closer to the sun and that when Earth formed it pushed Mars back and Venus forward sort of wedging itself into place between the two elder planets. Though this theory shouldn't have really effected Mars and Venus on a large scale as the Earth isn't that much younger, less than a billion years if science is right, which it usually is. If this city was on Mars' surface at that time, no one would have survived. Mars lost its atmosphere nearly instantly. That is, if it had an atmosphere by that time. Bear in mind, Earth was lifeless for two billion years as the planet cooled and began an atmosphere." Helga thought for a moment, but Kevin then interjected, "That doesn't explain how the city was buried so deep though."

Richard asked, "A billion years, surely that can bury a city with dust storms and what not even if there aren't any earthquakes here?"

Juliet nodded and Helga spoke up. "The oldest rocks we've discovered have only been around 3.2 billion years old on the surface. I can see how dust storms can bury an uninhabited city over the span of 4.6 billion years. But how can a civilization become advanced enough to grow and evolve to a level beyond us, next to us, before our planet even existed? This Solar system was created roughly 4.6 to five billion years ago." Juliet had had enough of this. "Enough, we are only half way there and have third hand information, and not exactly that much information. Let's stave off anymore theorizing until we get there."

There were nods of agreement, Kevin and Helga sat back in their chairs and Richard just chuckled while driving on.

CHAPTER 13

Cartwright and Capperman were walking down the hall towards the dig site. They had just finished Cartwright's orientation to the new recruits and Capperman received confirmation that the Mole team had arrived and departed for their mission.

Suddenly, Capperman's radio beeped, "Capperman here, go ahead."

"McAllen here, sir, where are you? I have urgent news for you and the General."

Cartwright looked at him and nodded, "We're in junction hall 37b section 3"

"Please don't move, sirs, I'll be there in a second!"

A few moments later, McAllen came running thru the hall and came to an abrupt halt at the two men slightly out of breath.

"That was fast McAllen, what can I do for you?" Cartwright said.

McAllen turned to the camera next to them and unplugged it. "Sirs, Frontier Colony hacked into the prison comms and CCTV."

Capperman quickly went from cheerful to upset but Cartwright merely grinned. "Comms was right on time, but I gotta hand it to them, the CCTV was good. My speech was on an open channel just for them. They will be coming to save the Fallok boy. Too bad it'll be too late."

McAllen was stunned. "Um, sir, may I ask what's up?"

Cartwright chuckled. "Sure thing McAllen. Fallok is sending a black ops team here to try and rescue his boy. He was going to from the off, but now that he knows we will be torturing him tomorrow, he's gonna rush a team here. He's gonna be emotional and sloppy and too late. Al-Rashar will be starting in an hour on him, only those signing up for then class knows."

McAllen and Capperman looked at Cartwright and smiled. "You're a genius Eric. You knew they would do this so perfectly." Capperman said with admiration in his voice.

Cartwright replied, "Naturally. Oh, when they launch whatever they use to get here, let it pass. I want them too far from home to get help." Cartwright's eyes widened with his smile.

The two men nodded at him and walked off. Cartwright then headed to his new quarters, the guest quarters previously occupied by Dustin Fallok. He radioed for Sergeant Farmer to meet him there; it had been a long day.

* * *

Blackness, he wasn't sure if his eyes were open or shut, all he could see was blackness. He felt something cold against his wrists, ankles, neck, and waist and felt a draft on his chest. His shirt and pants were off. He was strapped to a cold chair. But he still wasn't sure if the room was dark or if his eyes were shut. He felt like they were open but he just didn't know. That's when he heard the whisper coming in his ear.

"Hello Dustin. Comfy? I know I am. Here, allow me to shine some light on the situation." With that, he felt a cloth on his head; he noticed it was going up. Bright light was now all he could see.

"What do you want? Who are you?" He asked.

A new voice came in, attached to this new voice was a body now stepping forward, blocking some of the light. "I am Al-Rashar Kasim Abdullah. This other man with us is my pupil of two years, David Ossley. We are here to recruit you for the great army of The New United Earth Force. Yes I know it needs a better name than that." Al-Rashar turned toward Ossley, "Two men are amazing with tactical planning and orchestrating coups but they can't come up with an original name for their movement."

Dustin tried as hard as he could, but a small chuckle came out of his mouth at Rashar's joke. Next thing he knew he was on the floor face first still strapped to the cold chair which he now realized was very heavy.

* * *

Rashar and his pupil left the room, making sure to turn the lights off before exiting and leaving Dustin in that very uncomfortable position. As Rashar stepped into the back room to look at his class he surveyed the people. Most were from Hawkeye battalion, a few were former inmates such as Rashar and Ossley were, and yet there were a few who were recruits from the captured ships.

A lot of those members were hard to read, Rashar, and he surmised most of Hawkeye, were unsure of these people, they had been prisoners faced with an ultimatum of die or work for Cartwright. They had no real loyalty to the movement. They would have some tests to face, later. Now was time for introductions for himself, his students, and the class and lesson. Twenty minutes later he and Ossley walked back into the Lab.

* * *

It felt like hours sitting there, strapped to a metal chair that had to be double his weight, face first into the floor in the dark, cold room. Wearing nothing but his boxer briefs. He hadn't had anything to eat or drink since he was home. He had arrived and went straight to the dig site, too excited for anything else and thinking he would just get a bite when he needed to. By now he was well rested, he wasn't even sure how long he was knocked out, all he remembered was the sound of an explosion, then waking up to those two.

The door opened and the lights came on, Ossley and Abdullah stepped inside the room. Another man entered and at Abdullah's nod, lifted Dustin back into a more comfortable position. "Is that better Mr. Fallok?" Abdullah asked. Dustin didn't budge.

"Ah, I see, you think you will be tough yes? Well, I guess we will have to fix that. Do you know why you are in here?" Dustin just sat there staring at Abdullah.

"You are here because we would like you to join our cause."

This caught Dustin off. "You what?" he asked.

Ossley laughed as did Abdullah. "Is it that hard to believe Mr. Fallok? Yes, we want you to join us. We have a vision for humanity and the colonies. We only wish to make humanity better, but we also need allies on Mars to help us with that goal. General Cartwright would like you to be our first ally here. Oh and he would like to know what is hidden in that hole you buried." Dustin spit at the floor.

"Well, it seems he was right, you would be a bit of a challenge. Well, no worries, David, if you will please, I'm told our young friend here is a lefty, so we shall start with his right pointer."

Ossley nodded and pulled out a knife from a table that Dustin had only just noticed. His eyes went wide as Ossley approached with the blade. He wiggled to try and get free but to no avail. Next he tried to make a fist but it was too late, the other man grabbed Dustin's hand and held out his fingers.

Separating the pointer from the rest of the fingers, the third man held the finger firmly, Ossley brought the knife to the knuckle connecting Dustin's pointer finger to his hand, brought the blade under the finger facing up and began cutting. Dustin let out a horrific scream.

* * *

Walking down a hall on her way to see Eguia, Corporal Maria Jensan heard screams. She thru her hands up to her ears and quickened her pace. She passed Lieutenant McAllister, one of Farmer's men who stopped her. "Jensan, something wrong?" He asked with a smirk.

"N-no s-sir. Everything is f-fine." McAllister came closer to her and replied,

"Really? Then why cover your ears? Don't like the sounds of recruitment?"

"N-no sir, I-I'm not too fond of that sound."

"I see," McAllister said with a chuckle. "Come with me then Jensan let me help you get over this."

She backed away slowly, shaking her head. "N-no s-sir, please, please let me just carry on with my duties."

He approached her, she backed into a wall, and she had nowhere to go now. "Nonsense, Jensan, we're all a team, let me help you," he said with a big smile. Then he grabbed her and dragged her closer to the screaming. By now, Jensan had begun screaming in protest and was trying to escape McAllister's hold. He threw her against a wall where she hit her head and fell to the floor unconscious. He picked her up and slung her over his shoulder.

* * *

"Well, well, well, Mr. Fallok, you are a strong willed individual." Abdullah said as Ossley finished removing Dustin's pinky.

He was out of fingers on his right hand, a thumb and palm were all that remained. "Still nothing, Mr. Fallok?"

Dustin hadn't said anything, just screaming to the point of exhaustion. He had passed out twice from the pain only to be awoken by a bucket of ice cold water. Cut slowly, seal the wound with a mini laser torch and see if he speaks. If not, then move onto the next finger and repeat.

Four times now Dustin had gone through this and not once. He never said anything beyond a scream of pain. Suddenly there was a knock at the door. With Ossley and the third man standing over Dustin, Abdullah went to the door and opened it. It took a moment with his old and frail body so Dustin took this time to enjoy the reprieve.

When Abdullah finally opened it, there was a tall and muscular man standing there in marine garb with a woman in air force garb unconscious over his shoulder.

"Mr. Abdullah sir, I am Lieutenant Denis McAllister, I have a crewman here, one of our first recruits who needs a reminder of why she is here. She doesn't like screaming."

Both men smiled, and then Abdullah asked, "Is she expendable?"

McAllister nodded and Abdullah signaled for Ossley to grab another chair opposite from Dustin. They strapped her in and McAllister left the room.

A few moments later there was another knock on the door. This time it was a soldier with a food cart. The soldier and Abdullah's assistant set up a table between Dustin and Jensan and began eating. Ossley turned to Dustin after a moment. "Are ya hungry buddy? You want some food?"

Dustin was starving; of course he wanted some of that. It looked like the prison food made here, but it was something. He knew what the price would be though for food so he just closed his eyes, maybe he'd be allowed to take a nap while they ate. Ossley then walked over to Jensan and slapped her across the face.

* * *

A sharp pain to her face, she opened her eyes. "What happened?" she said, then she saw three men standing around and a fourth strapped to a chair covered in blood and soaked missing fingers on one hand and food on a table between her and the trapped man.

Suddenly the middle-aged man standing and facing her spoke, "Name, rank, position and loyalties. Now!"

She started stuttering and panicking; she was terrified for her life. "Ma-Maria Je-Jensan. C-Corp-poral. P-pilot f-for p-prison-n t-t-transport. H-hawkeye o-of c-course."

The middle-aged man laughed, as did his colleagues. She noticed Lieutenant Fasid with the middle-aged man and another very old middle-eastern man. This must be Al-Rashar Abdullah she thought to herself. And this must be his student, the middle-aged man.

"You aren't truly loyal to General Cartwright, Corporal," the man said with emphasis on her rank. "You are merely doing what you can to stay alive until you can escape or do some damage to our movement."

Jensan's eyes went wide, she started shaking her head violently. "No, no, it's not true, I'm loyal, I swear I'm loyal!" she proclaimed.

Then the other man in the chair looked up at the man. "Ossley, leave her alone. Or have you grown tired of torturing me so you had to get a weaker mind?" the man said weakly.

The middle-aged man, now known as Ossley turned around to the seated prisoner. "Oh, no, Fallok," said Ossley with a grin, "I've barely begun with you. She is just some fun for me. Why? Do you like her? She is very pretty. Though it must be hard for you to tell from so far away, and with her clothes on."

Jensan was even more scared now, she knew where this was going. Fallok's eyes went wide as well. "No! Don't do anything to her!"

Abdullah then chimed in, "Does that mean you will tell us what we want to know Mr. Fallok?"

* * *

Dustin was stuck, he couldn't tell them, but he couldn't let this innocent young woman get tortured or worse on his behalf. In his silence, Ossley brought his knife to Jensan's neck, grabbed her shirt and tore her jumpsuit all the way down. Dustin shut his eyes and tried to turn away. Next he heard an ear splitting scream, he opened his eyes to see what happened, against his better judgement. Her clothes had been torn off now and Ossley was on her.

"Ah, it's been too long for me."

Dustin couldn't bear watching that poor woman being violated by that monster of a man. He'd had enough. "Okay, I'll talk! Just stop!"

David Ossley rose off the woman and frowned, pushing her to the floor, still strapped to the chair. "I was having fun. You sure you wanna talk now? Don't you want to have some fun too?"

Dustin glared at him a moment, then turned to Al-Rashar. "I'll tell you what we were doing, but get him away from her, and put her back upright. Oh, and give her something to cover up."

Abdullah nodded. Ossley stepped closer to him and the third man went to Jensan to do as Dustin had ordered. "Okay, Mr. Fallok, I did as you asked. Now, what were you digging for?"

Dustin slumped his head down. "I got a message Thursday that I needed to come right away, we were drilling for a new mine for metals and ore to export to Earth and they had hit something that broke a drill. A metal stronger than anything naturally found on Earth or Luna. I came straight over after filing my report and requesting permissions. My monthly inspection of here was only two days away anyways. When I arrived I went straight to the site. Conferring with Warden Rodriguez en route. Once I arrived I first looked at the camera footage from the drill head. The metal wasn't natural, and it wasn't anything human made."

Abdullah seemed very interested, he asked, "Did you send a team down to examine it in person?" Dustin nodded. "What did they find?"

Dustin decided he'd told them enough. "I don't know." He started laughing at this. "I don't know," he repeated while he was laughing.

Everyone looked to each other and Abdullah asked, "What do you mean you don't know?"

Dustin stared at Abdullah and nodded his head towards the soldier. "They launched their attack. We buried the hole. Trapped our team down there and destroyed the computers to hide it all. Had Cartwright arrived a day later, we would have known a ton more about what was down there."

Dustin started laughing again. The irony of all of this was hilarious to him. And the looks on their faces was just as amusing.

Abdullah then asked, "As a scientist, what do you think it is?" Dustin laughed again. "You fools, I'm not a scientist. I'm a politician's assistant. I only know the very basics of science from school and what my parents taught me. My parents are the only scientists in the family."

"Then why were you overseeing the project?" Ossley asked. Dustin laughed again.

"I wasn't overseeing the project. I was there as a representative of the Martian government to learn about the discovery and report it back to my superiors. The scientists were the ones who went down the hole."

"Do you have any idea what it could be though?" asked Abdullah.

"It's some kind of structure. I have no clue what just that if it's that deep and that strong, it's been there for millenniums. And it was put down there on purpose."

Ossley spoke up now, "On purpose? You mean like aliens?" Dustin nodded. "But wouldn't it have been broken up and pushed down there over the years by earthquakes and age and stuff?" Dustin shook his head.

"No, Mars doesn't have tectonic plates. Sand storms could have covered it over time, but not bury it that deep. No, it was built down there." Abdullah went to the door, opened it and walked outside the room.

Ten minutes later he walked back in. This time with another person by his side. A tall, menacing and bulky man, he surveyed the room for a moment, looked at the covered woman who had cried until she passed out.

Then he stepped over to Dustin, looked at his right hand then back at him. "Good evening Mr. Fallok. I'm Colonel John Capperman. Abdullah tells me you've told them everything you know about the dig site, yes?"

Dustin nodded.

"Well done. I thank you for that. And for working so nicely with us, I'm authorized to make you an offer. Join our cause and you and Corporal Jensan there are free to go. We'll give you both medical treatment and even fit you with a prosthetic hand."

Dustin looked at Capperman. "Why would I want to join you? Your goal is to destroy humanity and the colonies."

Capperman smiled a sinister smiled like that of a door-to-door salesman in one of those old movies trying to sell a lemon to a homemaker. "Dustin—may I call you Dustin?" Capperman asked but didn't let him answer as he continued, "You clearly don't know anything about us or our views and goals. Humanity is corrupt and over populated. Our home world, Earth, has been suffering from overpopulation of humanity and heavy depletion of its natural resources for over a hundred years. We are merely seeking to help Mother Earth. Surely Earth and Humanity can survive better without six billion of its nearly 12 billion people."

It was clear that he believed this, but Dustin was still totally stunned, such a thing would be near genocide. Capperman clearly wasn't done either.

"As for resources, while I know Mars exports metal, we are low on food and space and a lot of that has been exported to Mars and Luna."

Dustin had to reply to this, he had to defend his people somehow. "What about all the good we have done for Earth? We bring people out here for Jobs. Half a billion people have moved to Mars, Luna, the Asteroid mines, and space stations over the last 25 years. Mars is almost self-sufficient as well, our farms grow quite a lot. Though visitors do miss meat while they're here."

Capperman nodded and said, "Yes, yes, imitations can only go so far. Have you ever had real meat?"

Dustin was enjoying this. Calm, easy conversation, keeping Capperman distracted. He wondered how long he could keep this up. "Last time I visited my Great Aunt Kathy and her family. About five years ago I think, it was Thanksgiving."

Capperman smiled, turned and then came back around and smacked Dustin. "Yeah, lie to me, great way to show you are a friend! I know for a fact you haven't been to Earth since you were four years old, when your family left

Earth and never returned. Like so many of your constituents. You all think Mars is better than Earth!"

Dustin shook off the hit, stared back at Capperman and said, "Native Martians aren't allowed on Earth, population issues. And anyone who lives on Mars or Luna more than five years is not allowed to return except on rare instances or for a visit with family of no more than one month for Lunars and three months for Martians. Your government's way of quelling overpopulation without killing people."

Capperman smiled at this, nodding his head in agreement. "Don't you see, Dustin? If we were to lower Earth's population, you and your people could return to their homes on good old Terra Firma."

Dustin shook his head. "No, not at the cost of billions of others. Mars is my home and I will defend it with my life."

Capperman shook his head and turned toward the door. He stopped just at the door, turned back to Dustin and said, "I accept that you won't join us. But we will still make our offer to those in the colonies, starting with Frontier, your home." He took a couple steps closer to Jensan. "Please, Dustin, tell us about Frontier's defenses, and any other secrets your office is privy to." Dustin shook his head as he said no to Capperman.

"Are you sure? Because if you don't, we might just have to take it out on young Ms. Jensan here. After all, we know you are very strong willed, and won't break to torture on you. But obviously you care too deeply for the innocent to watch one get harmed because of you."

Dustin kept shaking his head. "No, no I can't, too many people are depending on me. I can't save one life for the sake of thousands."

Capperman shook his head some more as he headed to the door. Before he stepped out he said to Abdullah, "Make it slow for her, slow and painful. And don't touch him anymore."

Turning to Dustin he said, "Oh, and Dustin, my good boy. You are a very brave man, you would have done so well with us. A pity though that this innocent young woman who only dreamed of flying through the stars will now have to die because of you. Her blood and that of your people will be on your hands now and forever."

With that, Capperman walked out the door. Dustin just kept shaking his head, repeating, "No" and "I can't". Ossley stepped over to Jensan who had awoken moments earlier. David Ossley picked up a small saw off of the table next to Jensan, went to her left wrist and began slowly sawing her hand off.

As Capperman marched down the hallway at a calm and slow pace, the screaming started. Throughout the prison, people stopped what they were doing for a moment as they heard the loudest and most terrifying sound many had ever heard.

And it lasted for hours.

CHAPTER 14

Joe was checking the sensors; they would be there in 45 minutes. "Okay, people, start getting ready, we are go in 45 minutes."

Everyone in the Mole, save for Jeremy who was driving, got up, started eating and then prepping their gear. Gas masks, breathers, each man had a SRL-100 plus their standard issue pulse pistols. Joe then reviewed the plan with everyone, it should be about 0400 for the prison. Though they weren't going to assume most people would be asleep.

From Jacob's last transmission burst, they had a general idea where Dustin was being held. The CCTV hack had been discovered so they were blind while they looked for a new way in. All communications had been placed on another band with rotating frequency. Jacob wasn't having any luck finding it so far.

Fostrell and Jeremy switched so Jeremy could get ready and then he moved the Mole into position at the dig site, it had been decided that that would make the least sound and had the least people around. At Joe's signal they went up.

Once out of the hole, they parked and took a look at their surroundings before exiting. A woman was approaching, she seemed upset. Joe turned on the outside mic to hear what she was saying.

"Dammit Ian! What the hell are you doing back so soon? You were supposed to report from down there! Get your ass out here now so I can shove your ass to General Cartwright. Oh I'm gonna enjoy watching him kill you for failing," she said with an evil glare.

Smiling, Joe stepped to the exit and opened the door, he hopped out stepped to the front and faced the fiery woman. When she saw it wasn't one of her people she started to back away slowly. "You're not Ian," she said. Her hand started moving to her radio but Marshals shot her with his SRL before she had the chance to do anything.

"No, I'm not," said Joe as Marshals and Fostrell came up behind Joe and swooped up the body, knowing she would be the first to awaken and sound an alarm, the two men thru her down the hole ensuring to strip her of her gear beforehand.

As the team made their way thru the twists and turns of the prison, ensuring to either silently knock out or avoid any hostiles, they finally found what they thought was the room Dustin was being held in. There were two guards outside the door, taking either side of the hall, Joe and Marshals sniped the guards rendering them unconscious. Jeremy and Fostrell ran up to the door to break the lock and ensure the marks were out cold while Joe and Marshals set up tripwire traps at the three ways to the room.

Jeremy got the door opened rather quickly and turned to the guards to drag them in, Marshals and Fostrell entered first to subdue any other hostiles inside the room.

A moment later Marshals came back out with his head slumped. "It's not pretty, sir, I think we're too late." Joe rushed in, pushing Marshals and Jeremy out of his way, the two grabbed the guards to bring into the room.

Joe stepped in, on one side of the room, Fostrell was vomiting. He looked at the center of the room. There were two chairs, Dustin was in one, unconscious, he was still alive, but his right hand was missing all four fingers and he was covered in vomit, tears, and blood. In the other chair were, body parts, the torso of a woman. The arms, hands, legs, and feet were all separated lying where they had dropped. Turning away, Joe noticed what was on the table between the two chairs, the woman's head. Covered in tears and blood, suspended in the shocked pose she had when she died.

After dropping the bodies of the guards to one side of the room, Jeremy looked at the gruesome scene and turned to vomit. Joe went to Dustin. "Dustin," he said, and began gently shaking him. "Dustin, wake up, it's Joe. I'm here to get you out of here."

Dustin opened his eyes. One look at Joe, and Dustin began shaking violently. "No, no, I'm dreaming, you're not here, you can't be here!"

Joe, smiled, he was alive. "Dustin, it's no dream, I'm here to rescue you. Have you told them anything?"

Dustin shook his head. "They did this to her, Joe you have to leave, they kept her alive until they finally removed her head, last. Made me watch the whole time. Get out of here while you can."

Joe was stunned, these people were monsters. He had to focus though. "Dustin, did you tell them about our defenses?"

Dustin looked at Joe, then at his team and replied. "No, nothing about Frontier, but Joe, leave, fast. He knew you were coming, it's a trap. Leave before you're all dead."

There was an explosion outside of the room, someone had tripped one of the wires. Joe signaled Fostrell and Marshals to go outside and clear a path for them. As they went, Joe unstrapped Dustin and he and Jeremy lifted Dustin onto his feet and helped him outside of the room. Joe stepped out of the room and didn't see either of his men, until he looked down, and saw them on the ground, holes in their heads.

Next moment, Dustin got heavier on his shoulders, Joe looked to Jeremy. She was on the ground, but not dead. Then he saw them—troops in every hallway, approaching slowly with guns raised, all pointing at him.

"Hold your fire, we want him alive." A man said from the left hallway, behind some men, but not for long as he slowly made his way thru the group of grunts.

"Well, well, well, Captain Joseph Ferguson isn't it?" Joe didn't move, he just stared hard at this man. Noticing the scar on his left cheek, Joe suddenly knew who he was face to face with. "I'm General—"

"Eric Cartwright," Joe finished.

Eric smiled and nodded. He signaled for everyone to lower their guns, four men came closer from the front hall and parted into pairs as they lifted and took away Miranda Jeremy and Dustin. Two more men came up behind Joe from the right hallway, one placing handcuffs on him, while the other searched and removed his gear. Joseph was stunned, this entire operation had been one of Cartwright's tricks. And Jacob and he had fallen for it; hook, line and sinker.

Cartwright continued his talking, "My apologies, Captain Ferguson, for leading you on and for the death of your men, but I'm sure you would have done the same. Though I do like these fancy new toys you have," he said while looking over an SRL one of his men handed him.

"New type of laser rifle I see, and from what I can tell, it's non-lethal. Very nice. Does that make it safe to fire near a dome?" Joseph didn't answer. "Oh, I think I see where Dustin here learned how to stay quiet. Well don't worry my friend, everyone talks. You did see Corporal Jensan in the interview room yes?"

Joseph's eyes went wide, he didn't need to look back to recall how that poor woman looked. "You're a monster." He said, "What on Earth did that woman do to deserve such a horrific death?"

Eric smiled at this, he approached Joseph and then peered into the room and turned back to Joseph. "Nothing really, she just didn't like screams. And it's actually Mr. Fallok who is to blame here. Turns out, he hates to see the innocent suffer. You know, you should be proud of the young man. We cut off, quite slowly too, each of his fingers on his right hand. He didn't say a single thing, of interest, quite a few jokes though. But low and behold, the moment my people went to work on Ms. Jensan, he spoke. Though he never did say anything about Frontier Colony, just the hole near where you came out of."

Joe was happy Dustin was so strong willed, but the toll of this night, would never go away. Provided they live through this. "Poor Jensan, Dustin never budged throughout her entire ordeal, in the end, she was begging us to kill her. But enough chatting here in the hallway. I should thank you for giving us another Mole to invade Frontier with. Now, we're gonna go let you join Dustin for a bit, to catch up and all, while we go have a nice little chat with that little cutie you brought with you," Cartwright said in reference to Jeremy.

The men dragged Joseph Ferguson away and moments later he was in a room with Dustin. He knew Jeremy was as good as dead, she didn't know anything, had nothing to bargain for.

* * *

"Well, that went rather well," Eric Cartwright said to Capperman as they walked down the corridor. "Time for the next phase, John, take McAllen, Farmer, and McAllister to Frontier Colony. Let's get this invasion started." Capperman nodded and walked off, radioing his team to meet up at the Mole.

As the team set off in the Mole, they found Lieutenant My Ya Jing inside the tunnel, trying to get out. After barely dodging the Lieutenant, Capperman descended from the Mole, "So you got thrown out like the trash by those guys eh Jing?" The petit Asian woman nodded slowly. Capperman smiled, "The General will not be happy about your failure. I suggest you come with us to redeem yourself."

Jing looked up to Capperman, "Where are you going?" She asked.

"Frontier Colony, to scout out the terrain and do some sabotage for the invasion." Jing nodded to accept the mission and headed into the Mole with Capperman hot on her tail. Once inside he took his seat at navigation, Jing looked around but all of the seats were taken, "The floor Jing, failures don't get seats." Capperman said. Jing sat on the floor between everyone, McAllen then switched the Mole into gear and resumed course, for victory.

CHAPTER 15

I an was bored, they'd been in this machine just sitting and moving at a snail's pace for what felt like ever. Suddenly Raul called out, "We're approaching the coordinates, people." Everyone sat up and looked front at the dashboard. Moments later, they broke thru the rock wall ahead and saw a cavern, but then tipped.

"Stop! Stop!" Susan called out but it was too late, they were in a free fall. The Mole hit the ground beneath and rolled over, it was built strong enough that the impact hadn't caused an explosion, but it did sustain heavy damage. The power was out in the cabin, Ian felt for his flashlight, releasing it from his belt he turned it on. They were upside down, thank goodness for seatbelts, he thought to himself.

Ian released his buckle and fell to the ceiling, he turned to the chair beside him. "Doctor Groeneg, are you alright?" he said as he began looking over her head and body for any injuries.

The light in her face helped wake her up. "Yes, yes I think I'm okay, a bit light headed though," she said.

Susan and Raul were stirring and slowly getting out of their chairs, getting to the ceiling a bit more elegantly than Ian had. "Okay, hold onto my shoulders, I'm going to release you from your seatbelt and ease you down. Okay?" She nodded to him and slowly he released her and helped her flip to the ceiling. Susan went to the hatch and was about to open it when Raul called out to stop.

Groeneg then said, "We need to put on the EVA suits, there's no atmosphere down here, remember."

Susan looked down, she felt like an idiot almost killing them all for a stupid mistake. Everyone had suited up and checked their internal systems and equipment to ensure they had not suffered any damage, everything was surprisingly well protected. Susan went for her second attempt to open the hatch, she stepped out first. The positive side of being upside down was that the ground was much closer to the hatch door.

Though it would be a climb getting back in at just over a meter.

After everyone got out of the Mole, Susan went to take a perimeter search and recon, Raul and Ian went to look at the external damage to their means of escape from the pits of Mars, and Dr. Groeneg just stared at everything. This was a truly inspiring discovery indeed. Susan quickly came back to the team. "We aren't alone down here." She said quickly, "Group of four coming towards us."

Ian seemed worried. "Could it be an interception team from Frontier? How could they beat us here? How could they even know where we were going?" he asked in a panic.

Groeneg shook her head. "No, Captain, it's got to be the scientists that were trapped down here. There was a chance that they had survived the cave-in. They must have heard the crash and are coming over to help and hoping we will help them out."

Susan smiled. "Captain, may I suggest we pretend we are from Frontier to get them to cooperate with us?"

Ian shook his head. "No," he said. "They must know about things on Frontier we don't know. We'll say we are from Red Colony. That we have taken command of this dig site because Frontier wasn't supposed to be so secretive of such a discovery."

Susan smiled, came over and hugged Ian. When she finished her embrace she said, "You are such a genius when you want to be my darling." Everyone was slightly caught off guard by this sudden sweetness by the toughest member of the group.

A few minutes later, four people approached them in similar EVA suits. The leader called out, "Hey! It's about time you got here! What the hell happened? We were nearly killed!"

Ian approached the man in as friendly yet military like way as possible. "I'm sorry, Doctor, we had some difficulties. Are you aware of what has happened on the surface?"

The leader shook his head and replied, "No, there's little to no signal for communications to work down here, had there been, we would have been able to warn you of the drop down here. Though that is how we escaped the cave in. The high ceilings gave us enough warning to get to cover in one of the buildings."

Everyone had been staring about, but at mention of buildings, all eyes were on this man. Groeneg replied, "Excuse me, but you said buildings?"

The man nodded. "Yes, didn't Dustin Fallok tell you? It was all in our last report. We found elements of alien made structures. This is an alien city from before the creation of Earth."

Jaws dropped all over, but that's when the scientists became suspicious. "You are from Dustin's team aren't you? Or at least from Frontier Colony, yes?"

Ian replied as diplomatically as he could. "I'm sorry, Doctor, but no we are not. We are from Red Colony. My bosses found out about a historic discovery here. They couldn't allow for more prosperity to go purely to Frontier Colony, it already makes three times as much progress as Red and Kwying Ma. But rest assured, you are still leading this expedition, we are merely here to assist and then extraction."

"And what about the cave-in?!" Burst out one of the other scientists.

Ian replied, "Dustin Fallok's misguided attempt to hide the discovery us. Now please, what lead you to this thought that this city? Is from before our very planet was created?"

One of the scientists shook his head. "Not before Mars, before Earth."

Ian looked at the man. "Earth is what I was referring to, Doctor. We are new to this planet, it is not ours, but belongs to those who once dwelled in here," he said opening his arms to the city beyond them.

This silenced the man, the lead doctor continued, "In one of the buildings, we saw a map of the solar system. Venus was further from the sun, Mars closer, almost where Earth is now. Pluto wasn't even a moon of Neptune yet and there was no Asteroid field."

Another doctor nudged him. "Oh, also the two moons of Mars were further from Mars' orbit and at least twice the size they are now."

Ian looked to his own team, this was indeed shocking news. Our Earth was one of the youngest planets in the Solar System, and a civilization lived on Mars before Earth was even around.

Groeneg asked then, "Have you found out what happened here? Or how our planet was formed?"

The lead doctor shook his head. "Not yet," he said, "but you're here so we can split up and search for more answers.

CHAPTER 16

K orskiev was nearing the coordinates. "Let's go down here," he said to Romo.

Romo looked to his superior, "But, sir, our coordinates are still a kilometer away."

Korskiev looked at Romo with a stern "don't you dare question me" stare. "I am well aware of that, Lieutenant. But I don't feel much like driving into an ambush unless I know I will win. You will bring us in here so we can get into whatever shafts we are looking for and surprise the enemy."

Romo nodded to his superior and complied with the order, as they steered down deeper, a quarter of a kilometer; they broke thru a wall and fell. Launching the emergency parachutes, the Mole landed on its feet and moved forward a few meters before coming to a halt.

Koskiev radioed the second Mole to be careful of the drop. "Thank goodness for the parachutes Jacob added to these thing at the last minute."

Romo said, "It wouldn't have been pretty if we had one of the first models of Moles on this trip." Moments later, the second Mole came to an elegant landing just behind team 1.

Richard Granit exited first, followed by Kevin Daniels who turned to assist Doctors Johannesburg and Fallok. Richard came over to team 1. "Sir, Team 2 is good and in high spirits. And between us sir, I think I should be given a Doctorate just for listening to 12 hours of science talk."

Team 1 gave a hardy laugh to this and Korskiev gave Granit a firm pat on the back and said, "Maybe when we get out of this place Lieutenant." The rest of Team 2 made their way to Team 1's position.

"So what's your plan Commander?" Doctor Fallok asked. Romo was scanning for life around them while Katrolla and Harvet secured the perimeter and Moles from anyone not a member of their party. Daniels and Johannesburg were looking around trying not to get too far from the others, but the sites were amazing.

Romo came over then and said, "Commander, picking up eight life signs approximately .68 kilometers North by Northwest of our position."

Korskiev nodded to Romo, and then turned to Granit and Fallok. "Lt. Granit, you are to stay by Dr. Fallok's side and protect them, go where ever she needs but keep constant eye on the enemy's whereabouts as well as ours and stay away from them. We will go in pursuit of them and try to apprehend without bloodshed."

Richard asked to speak freely, Korskiev nodded and Richard said, "Sir, eight against four isn't very good odds."

Korskiev laughed. "I thought you learned something from your trip with these scientists. There will only be three soldiers max there."

At Richard's confused look, his CO continued, "There was a team of scientist down here already, we now know they are alive. They only took one Mole so there could only be four of Cartwright's people here. Since they did not know if the scientists were alive or not, they brought at least one of their own. They must be a CO, scientist, technician, and one grunt. We outnumber them just with our first team. That was the whole point of two teams."

Richard nodded and Korskiev rounded up his team to head out.

Richard gathered up his team to give out his words of inspiration. This took a good few minutes as everyone had been so fascinated by the sites that they kept wondering off. "I have been placed in charge of your protection, however, there is only one of me, and three of you. So I need you to help me, help you. How? I need you to all stay together, no wondering off. No splitting up unless I have already assessed the risks of the second party's course.

"We arrived as four and we will leave as 4. Now I know this is all quite fascinating, but these rules are for your protection. This is still Doctor Fallok's operation so she will be determining where we go, but I have the right to stop us, turn us around, or to veto a direction based upon the risks. Also, tread carefully, I know if I had left a city buried this deep underground, I wouldn't leave it unguarded, so I will be jumping around from point to tail and back at any given time, and most importantly of all. If I give you an order, I need you to follow it, to the letter, right away. Hesitating is what gets people killed. Okay, any questions?" he finished with a smile.

No one asked any but Juliet took this time to make her address to the team. "Thank you, Richard, that was well said. And we all promise to obey your orders for our best chances of survival here. Though no more of this doctor nonsense, we are family and colleagues here, so you may refer to us on a first name basis."

The other two scientists smiled at this, while Richard nodded with an embarrassed frown. Juliet continued in her soft, calming tone. "As we are to steer clear of Team 1 and its mission, we will begin on the opposite direction, Richard, as you are constantly looking at sensor readings to assess life signs and any other hazards, I'd like you to map the city please. Just record your scans and it should link together to form a map."

Richard nodded and began typing in the necessary commands while listening to everyone else's responsibilities. "Kevin, I want you to record all findings as we go building to building. Especially any writings or forms of communication."

Kevin nodded to his orders and Juliet turned to Helga. "Helga, just keep your eyes peeled for any signs of technology and see what you can find out about the materials around us. Obviously I'll be assisting the two of you." She said pointing at her fellow scientists. Richard, she knew, wouldn't need her help and would ask if he had any inquiries.

With the huddle complete, Team 2 headed out in its direction. By this time, Team 1 had already gone out of sight, hidden by the unnatural structures, this underground jungle of ancient ruins.

* * *

Korskiev and his team had made it. They could see Cartwright's men and the scientists. Once Romo had set up the microphone, he was able to listen in on what was going on. From the voice and facial scans, Korskiev was able to identify Ian Slovski, Susan Vekle, Raul Geoffrey, and Doctor Elisabeth Groeneg in the Mole suits. From the report given to him by Jacob Fallok, the Exploration Team consisted of a Doctor Julian Broklor, Doctor Asa Garshari, Doctor Guten VanDurben, and Lieutenant Justin Shaffer as the team escort.

"It looks like Slovski has them convinced they are from Red Colony." Romo reported after listening for a bit. "Dr. Garshari is spilling the beans about everything they've learned sir," he continued.

Korskiev was thinking of a plan to get the scientists safe.

Turning to Romo he asked, "Can we enter Garshari or any of his other members' internal comms without Slovski's team noticing?"

Romo looked over the stats for the prison issue suits. "It's possible sir, but if our timing is off, Slovski or one of his people may notice someone isn't listening or is talking to someone else if they see mouths moving. Especially Lieutenant Shaffer; Vekle has been sticking close to Shaffer, she's definitely the muscle of the group so she's staying close to the other muscle so she can take him out when needed. My suggestion would be to contact VanDurben, they don't see him as much of a threat."

87

Harvet came over. "Sir, Dr. Groeneg seems nervous, the only reason we even knew she may have been with the Hawkeyes is because the transport she was on with her family never made it to Luna. I suspect she isn't here by choice. I think we should contact VanDurben and tell him to sense something from one of these buildings, bring all the scientists into a building and take care of escorts. Our only potential casualty maybe Shaffer unless we can get him a warning."

Romo nodded and said to Korskiev, "I think we can pull that off sir."

Korskiev agreed and selected a building. "Let's set up a protective field inside the building, Vekle or Shaffer may go inside first, let's try and make it Shaffer and get him out of harm's way."

Katrolla took point and Harvet took rear as the team headed to a building about ten meters from where there targets were talking. They quietly entered the building, Romo and Harvet began setting the trap while Katrolla covered the door in case someone heard them and approached before the trap was set. Korskiev went and explored the mysterious construct.

* * *

Doctor Guten VanDurben was seated on the edge of what was once a fountain, barely listening to Groeneg and Garshari talking about the city. VanDurben was the leader of the team when they left MMP but once they found that this was an archeological find and not a new mineable metal, he lost lead of the team, Metallurgic analysist was now second priority, Archeology had taken top spot, so it went to Dr. Garshari to lead the team now. VanDurben had no hard feelings of course, as it was natural and he was okay with it. But he didn't trust these people. He knew Dustin, and knew that Dustin wouldn't have risked killing them had it only been a jurisdiction issue. There was something else going on here he felt. And he didn't like it.

While Garshari spilled everything they had found to these strangers, he just sat there looking over his scans, waiting for them to move on to actual research. Suddenly, he no longer heard the people around him, he looked to his armband monitor to check the volume, it wouldn't be the first time he hit the mute key on this damn sensitive switch.

Suddenly, he heard a voice, "Doctor VanDurben, Yes? Please nod slightly, we do not wish you to draw attention to yourself or us." The voice said, to which VanDurben slightly moved his down as if trailing off, and quickly back up.

Anyone looking would merely assume he was fighting off sleep. Something to which everyone there was doing. "Good, thank you Doctor. We have secluded your comm from the others. Those men are not from Mars. They are members of Colonel Cartwright's Hawkeye Battalion. I am Commander Korskiev from Frontier Colony. Mars Maximum has fallen into his hands and Dustin Fallok covered the dig site to slow them down in coming here. We have set a trap for them in the following building." On his screen, a blip appeared at one of the local buildings.

"Just have your team come examine the sensor reading on your screen. If they insist on a security sweep, try and suggest your man to do it as he would know what to look for. I'd like to rescue all of you without any bloodshed."

VanDurben accepted the request, just then he felt a knock on his helmet. He looked up and saw the woman of the Hawkeye team, Vekle he recalled. She was saying something to him, VanDurben looked back to his wrist panel and changed back to the frequency.

Vekle repeated, "Who were you talking to? And why aren't you on our channel?"

VanDurben replied, "I'm sorry sir, I didn't realize I was on a different frequency. I was talking to all of you. I just found something on my sensor screen. It looks to be another type of element in a nearby building."

Vekle nodded and Garshari then interjected facing Slovski. "Apologies, Captain, Doctor VanDurben is constantly knocking his wrist band, it causes mutes and frequency changes often, on good instances."

Slovski nodded at Vekle and she backed from the scientist. Garshari then continued, "If VanDurben has found something we should check it out, sir."

Slovski nodded again and said, "Okay but we should do a security sweep of the building before any of you go in there."

The scientists nodded and then VanDurben added, "Lieutenant Shafer knows what to look for Captain, he does a sweep prior to every building, and we've run into a few traps so as I said, he knows what to look for." Slovski agreed but insisted Vekle Join him so that she could learn what to look for.

* * *

As the two soldiers stepped into the building, Shafer began explaining what to look for. They turned a corner, losing sight of the rest of the team still outside. As soon as they were out of sight, both helmet comms went off. Shafer was pushed to a wall as Vekle was jumped by three other figures. Going down almost instantly, Shafer looked at his attackers.

His comm went back on and he heard a new voice. "Hello, Lieutenant Shafer, I am Commander Korskiev from Frontier Colony. Your friend there is a member of Hawkeye Battalion. What can you tell us of the others in her company?"

"VanDurben was right not to trust them then. Their leader looks like a scared kid, named Ian. From what I can tell, he has no military background and is most likely a forced recruit. She—" She pointed to the now unconscious Vekle. "—is the strongest of the group, probably the muscle keeping them all in check. There is a scientist with them as well who is probably being forced here and then the last guy hasn't said anything, but I gathered he's genuine Hawkeye tech division. He has a hack kit with him."

Korskiev nodded at the report. "Thank you," he said. "Please signal for them to enter the building, we have unjammed your link." As each team member stepped around the corner, they were either hushed and placed to one side, or jammed and knocked to another side. Once all four Hawkeyes were conscious and bound in the corner, Korskiev began the interrogations.

CHAPTER 17

J acob was still trying to get the video feedback. With Cartwright onto him, holding a hack on the videos never lasted more than 30 seconds and it could take an hour to get anything back.

"Fostrell and Marshals' bio signs just dropped," called Rob from the other side of the command center.

Jacob pulled up the biosignatures to his monitor. Each member of the three teams had biosign chips on them though GPS was too risky do to the stealth level of their missions. A moment later, Jeremy's bio showed injury and Joe's extreme stress based upon heart and blood pressure.

"Damn, they must have been captured." Rob continued, "Jacob, we shouldn't have let Joe go on such a risky mission. Between Joe and Dustin, Cartwright will know everything."

Jacob banged his fists into the wall. With tears welling up in his eyes he said, "I know. We have to begin safe guarding the colony. I'll call up Chuck, we need to get that feed up

Jacob called Mayor Graleen to update him on the situation, recommending they begin evacuating everyone to their emergency bunkers or at least get near them and stand by. Following Joe's instructions should he be captured, the colonial defensive plan would be changed to plan B. A plan that Joe had been left out of to prevent the strategy from falling into enemy hands. Though the bunkers and secure access points couldn't change, once Jacob activated Plan B, the passcodes and security protocols and officers changed.

No one except for the computer program that Jacob and Rob had created knew prior to the deployment of Plan B, who those people would be or what the protocols would be. Security systems would change in frequency, severity, and pattern. Joseph's military and personal files would be transferred to Jacob's secure server at the command center and only become accessible at a certain terminal once Plan B was deactivated or Rob and Jacob put in both of their personal codes simultaneously at that and one of their consoles; the order changing daily.

Returning to the terminals after calling the mayor, Jacob announced, "Chuck has implemented Plan B and ordered all civilians to their emergency bunkers immediately. Rob, time for us to initiate our part and activate the distribution of the codes and protocols."

Rob and TR nodded compliance. Going to their stations, the two men pulled up the Plan B program and entered their codes, confirmations, and Joseph's biochip signature and location for program monitoring.

Three hours had gone by and the evacuation to the bunkers had been going smoothly. Jack checked in with Jacob over their secure link, he was still grounded but Tyler and he were sitting in their cockpits ready to fly the moment they received the all clear. Melissa just arrived in the command center after completing the evacuation and securing of her mother's labs. She took up her terminal, monitoring life support systems and bio signatures all over the colony including the bunkers.

The 3D holodisplay at her terminal allowed for her to view all levels of the colony and bunkers as well as scrolling, enlarging, shrinking, receiving and sending reports, announcements and signals all at the slightest twitches of her fingers. Working with Jacob's holoterminal, they could also isolate sections of the colony, lock them down to hold for authorities, or even extract the oxygen from certain compartments. This was planned only if the enemy managed to get into one of the access corridors to the bunkers. Some of Joseph's top officers would be arriving within the hour to assist with monitoring and dispatching operatives throughout the colony from this command center.

Melissa was looking at all of these heat signatures, knowing that each one was a person who had left their world behind at one point in their lives to come here, to live in peace. Now, they were living in fear, no idea what would happen tomorrow or how long they would be staying in these shelters. If they did exit would it be with their leaders or mass murderers greeting them at the doors. She was worried about Richard and her mother most of all though. Unsure what was happening down in that tunnel they went to.

She had grown up in an age of people being connected to each other via cyberspace. That had been the way of things for nearly a hundred years. Status, pictures, friends both near and far, and almost always connected to each other; her and Richard and mom. She'd never gone so long not talking with mom, and Richard, she spoke to him once a day at least since their engagement so many months ago and then marriage, since then it was twice a day plus every night. Even if they didn't speak directly, there was always status and walls.

Whoever came up with walls and status and all of that, had some great ideas but crazy names, she thought. Since leaving nearly 24 hours ago though, she hadn't heard from either of them. She couldn't even get a reading on their location, biochip signatures, or even a heat signature from the vicinity or depth they were supposedly at. It was just too deep and too far. Though the idea of too deep and too far when still on this planet seemed so laughable to Melissa as they could have live feeds and FaceTime video chats from Earth, Luna, the space stations, ships, and even asteroid mining compounds near Jupiter. Yet they couldn't get a single spec of anything from deep in this seemingly lonely planet. Her eyes became blurry as they swelled with tears on the verge of escaping down her face. She felt a hand on her should, followed by an arm around her. Looking to the owner of the arm, she saw her father.

"I miss them too honey. But we have to stay strong for our home." He said to her.

Melissa stifled her tears back and Jacob embraced her a bit stronger, catching her tears on his shirt. He held her for eternity it seemed like, until Rob interrupted.

"Jacob! Joe's Mole is moving! It just entered our sensor range!"

Melissa became excited but for a moment. When she looked to her father, he looked angry, serious, and stern. Not a glimmer of happiness that her uncle Joe was returning somehow with Dustin.

"Daddy, Joe succeeded!" she said, but Jacob just shook his head and began going back to his terminal as he replied.

"No, Mel, his signal is still at Mars Max, that Mole would have left about 20 minutes after his capture to be where it is now. That's an enemy scout team. Rob, has the base picked this up yet?"

Looking to his partner in this, rob nodded his head in the affirmative. "They're dispatching interception teams to destroy the Mole. General Decker's orders are to prevent a single Hawkeye from setting foot on the colonies. Whatever it takes."

CHAPTER 18

Capperman was sitting at the Nav controls, overlooking the distance left to the colony and depth of the mole. Suddenly there was an earthquake and the Nav screen began blaring alarms. "Multiple heat signatures and tremors." McAllan announced from the helm. Jing was holding onto whatever she could so as not to go flying around.

"Explosions. They know we're here." Capperman observed, "They're trying to bomb enough on the surface to hit us. A cave-in would barely slow us down."

McAllister called out, "But sir, how did they find us?"

Thinking a moment Capperman said, "There must be a GPS chip somewhere in here. The moment we were within range of the satellite they must have found us. I'm sure they know we aren't their Black Ops team, must have been tracking them as well. McAllen, dig deeper."

"But, sir!" McAllan said. "Even if we go deeper, they'll keep firing till they get us or be waiting wherever we enter the colony. We won't be able to find the GPS chip anytime soon."

Pulling up a holographic image on the miniature display terminal between their two seats. McAllan pulled up a schematic of the Mole. Enlarging on a section in the control consoles, McAllan highlighted the chip, and all of the critical systems surrounding it. "If we rushed to disable the GPS chip we'd hit life support, more specifically the heater, oxygen recycler, lighting, and either navigational controls or drive functioning depending on our route of access. If we take our time though it'll take four hours to reach it and we still won't be moving during that time. Either way we'd be a sitting duck or a cooked goose."

Nodding, Capperman asked for suggestions. Farmer suggested abandoning ship and walking the rest of the way. "But there's only four suits!" Jing exclaimed.

Farmer then said "Well then, we may get the GPS fixed after all."

Getting excited for her chances, Jing exclaimed, "Great idea! McAllan stay here!" Shoving Jing into her chair Farmer said, "Not quite Jing, he's more useful to us gaining access to the colony. You stay here. Catch up to us once you've lost those bombers." Everyone else had begun suiting up, Jing sat mortified.

"But I don't know how to take this thing apart!" McAllan came over with a smile and said, "Just have the computer tell you what to do. You're good at following orders. And this one is beneficial to you."

At her inquisitive look, he continued, "You can either fix this and join us, or not fix it and die or screw up and die. Three options for you, two not so nice ones. Have fun. Oh, and I'd suggest you go put an oxygen mask on before we open the hatch."

She sat there in shock as he said all this to her, but as Capperman went to unseal the hatch, Farmer kicked her off the chair and pointed to the mask in front of her. Jumping to the mask and securing it over her head just as Capperman opened the hatch and all of the air was sucked out of the cabin.

McAllan waved goodbye to Jing on his way out and then sealed the hatch back on the outside. Pulling up a holodisplay on his suit's wrist ban, he pointed in a direction. McAllister and Capperman slung their rifles and pulled two hand drills from an outside hatch on the Mole and began digging to the surface.

At their rate, McAllan had estimated it'd take two hours to reach the surface and then another six hours of walking to reach the colony's outer wall. EVA suits could last for 48 hours without stress, so they estimated each person would have between 24 and 36 hours depending on talking, person, and how well they handle this stage of their adventure.

CHAPTER 19

Sitting in the cell, more a torture chamber, Joseph Ferguson and Dustin Fallok sat and sat. They spoke little to each other as they weren't sure if they were being watched but assumed it most likely. Unsure how many hours they had been sitting in the cramped room, Joseph had been thoroughly searched, all that remained was his organic biochip that was implanted at birth.

Jacob had more than likely implemented Plan B when Fostrell and Harvet's chips showed them die. Jeremy though, Joseph was very worried about. She had more than likely been given medical treatment or was just sitting in another cell. Doubting that Cartwright would interrogate her when he was available, and Joseph had said from the start that she didn't know anything.

The lights turned up from a dim barely visible level to almost blinding, the door opened while Joseph and Dustin squinted in an attempt to adjust to the sudden change. A figure stepped in and thru a round object into Joseph's lap. Looking down he saw Miranda Jeremy's horrified face, hollowed eyes sockets staring back at him, lifeless.

Joseph jumped up letting the head of one of his best soldiers and a mother of two drop to the floor. "What the hell is this? How could you!" he screamed at the man in the doorway, no care for an actual answer from his anger.

The man stepped further inside the room, letting the shadows show his face, Cartwright replied, "You were right, she didn't know anything. Worth a try anyways. Ossley, take our friend Captain Ferguson to our interview room. It's his turn now."

Three men stepped into the room behind Cartwright. One stepped toward Dustin to ensure no attempts to protect Joseph while the other two grabbed Joseph by each arm and headed out of the room.

Cartwright followed behind them and as the last man was turning to leave, he picked up the head of his latest victim and set it next to Dustin. "There's another great dame for your collection. I enjoyed her more than Jensan. Let's see how well your Captain goes shall we?"

With that, Ossley began laughing as he headed out of the room. The door locking up behind him, Dustin now sat alone in the cell, just him and the head of Miranda Jeremy. A soldier whom he had worked closely with for many years. As dead as Jensan, and she had known it would happen after seeing Jensan before her capture.

Dustin felt so responsible for these deaths. He was overcome with sorrow. The will to live had left him. He made the decision, no one else should die over him. He stood up and ran to the door hitting it head-on and causing a loud noise as his head hit the clear, unbreakable graphene door. He fell to the floor from the rebound but stood up and did it again.

Outside, the two guards on the other side of the door watched as he repeatedly rammed into the door. Five, six times and he just kept doing it. His head had cracked on the second round but he just kept at it.

Another guard came running down the hall. "What the hell is wrong with you two? If he kills himself Cartwright will kill the both of you!" she screamed at them.

The two guards abruptly stopped laughing and opened the door. Dustin rammed into the first one knocking the both of them into the adjacent wall. As they both fell to the floor, Dustin grabbed the gun at one's waist and brought it to his head.

Looking up to the other two guards on their feet he exclaimed, "Stay back! I will do it!"

The new guard took aim with her gun, "The General said you needed to live. He didn't say shit about not wounding you."

Dustin looked straight at the guard and spit in her direction and replied, "Tell Cartwright, I'll never betray them. Fuck you!"

And he pulled the trigger.

CHAPTER 20

"**H**e's gone," Rob said. Jacob was engrossed in planning another way to fortify the colony. The bombers had reported no contact on the enemy Mole and it had been two hours since they began their bombardment.

"Did you say something Rob?" Jacob asked. Rob repeated it a bit louder. "Who's gone?"

"Dustin's lifesigns just peaked for a minute, then died. He's dead Jacob." They had been able to read Dustin's biochip since Joe arrived and enhanced his chips signal for monitoring by the command center.

Jacob fell to his knees. His oldest son was dead, how could that happen? Joseph was supposed to protect him.

"What's Joe's status?" He asked. Still on the floor. Melissa had also left her terminal at the news, she went to one of the cots nearby, crying her eyes out for her brother.

Rob replied, "A lot of stress, pain. I think they're torturing him. There is one thing about Dustin's death though."

Jacob looked at Rob quizzically. "He was calm, just before his death. Almost like he expected it."

Jacob stood up and started heading towards him asking, "What? Like an execution squad?"

Rob shook his head and said, "No, more like…" He paused a second to reconfirm, he resumed. "More like a suicide."

Jacob was stunned, he ran to Rob's terminal and asked, "You're sure it was suicide? Why would my boy commit suicide?" Jacob said. Then he looked to Rob, grabbing his friend by the collar he said, "Why would my boy kill himself!?"

Everyone in the command center had stopped what they were doing. Looking at Jacob Fallok as he broke down at the news.

Rob said, "I, I don't know. We don't know for sure what is going on there, only that people are dying. Jeremy died very painfully, and Joe's heart rate and endorphins have spiked just as hers did. I believe they're interrogating him now."

Jacob looked to his friend, still sobbing on the floor he asked, "Do you think Dustin was trying to avoid another round of interrogations?"

Looking down to Jacob, the two had gone thru so many things together for 45 years they'd been friends but this was the hardest moment of Rob's and

Jacob's lives. Nodding slowly to Jacob, and to himself. Rob knew that Dustin had a damn good reason for taking his own life. It was the only explanation he could give himself. Rob helped Jacob up to his feet and the two men went over to the cot that Melissa was lying on, crying for her dear departed brother. TR and some relief personnel Commander Lee had sent over were manning their stations.

"Mel?" Jacob said in a soothing voice as he took a seat at the edge of the cot. He rubbed her back gently in his way that always soothed her sorrows. He knew it wouldn't be nearly as effective today. He needed soothing himself but his kids were too close to each other, he had to force himself to be strong, for her sake if not for his own. Rob pulled up a chair beside them and just sat hunched over rubbing his eyes.

After a few minutes of sitting there, together, Rob asked Jacob if he wanted to tell Jack and Chuck himself. Rob had to ask a couple times as Jacob had just sat there with a blank stare and tears flowing. Jacob shook his head slowly and said as he slowly placed both hands on his knees and came up his feet. "No, I should do it. Jack needs to hear it from me."

As he got to his feet though, Melissa's arm grabbed his wrist. "Daddy, please stay with me a bit longer. I don't want to be alone right now."

Unable to deny his daughter's plea. He sat back down and rubbing his hand on her shoulder to help ease her.

Rob went over to the soldier at the communications terminal and returned moments later with a secure radio for Jacob. "Here," he said holding it in front of him, "it's already set to radio Jack. He needs to know."

Jacob took the handset from his friend's hand and hit the call signal. The holographic screen appeared above it and moments later Jacks face was staring at Jacob.

"Hi, Dad, what's the word?" Jack asked, serious but an air of confidence with him. Jacob just stared for a moment, thinking how much Jack and Dustin looked alike.

The brown hair with the receding hairline, the nose and cheeks. They both had big bright hazel eyes, a family trait that always showed eagerness and wonder in them. So many people used to mistaken them for twins, only a couple years a part. Jacob told him of his brother. Jack's face changed so quickly from quizzical to worry, to shock, and then to an anger that Jacob had never seen in his boy. Jack closed the channel.

Ten minutes later, Commander Lee was calling.

Rob answered, "Yes Commander, what can we do for you?"

She answered very sternly, "Where's Jacob! Jack's gone AWOL in one of my jets and he spoke to Jacob moments before!"

Turning the holoscreen towards Jacob, Rob just sat there looking to his friend who pulled his head up from his hands to look at the Commander who would now be in charge indefinitely. Getting Joe back was beginning to feel impossible.

"Jeez, Jacob, what did you tell Jack?"

Looking at her, he shook his clear then said opened his mouth to form the words. "Dustin is dead."

Lee turned from angry to shocked. She covered her mouth and tears began to swell, Lee and Dustin had been close friends and lovers once. Jacob then asked what Jack was doing.

"He overrode the security locks on his fighter and cleared the hanger then took off. Tyler is in pursuit but he silenced all comms. Now that I know what happened, he's probably going to do something stupid like attack the prison. And Tyler will either shoot him down or Join him." She said looking serious but burdened. She then asked, "I suppose you haven't called the Governor yet to update him have you?"

Rob turned the screen to him once more and said, "Not yet, but I'll call him next. Jacob needed to tell Jack first and he and Melissa need some time. I'll take care of whatever you need done here for the moment. Lieutenant Daniels' team is doing a fine Job here as well. We'll stay in contact."

Lee nodded and signed off. Rob turned and walked over to Lieutenant Daniels who had taken over at Jacob's monitoring terminal. Whispering to the head of the technical team he said, "Try and get us into Jack's cockpit. Find his co-pilot, and let's see what systems we can override ok?" With a nod by Daniels, Rob continued, "Use TR's skills for that, trust me when I say you'll need him."

With another nod by Daniels, Rob walked to his terminal and sent a secure signal to Governor Lorely Vaschev of the United Martian Colonies in Red Colony and informed her of the fate of her top aid. Rob's biggest regret would be not being able to inform Juliet Fallok of her eldest son for who knew how long.

Lt. Daniels then called over to Rob. "Dr. Bellington." Rob acknowledged to continue. "The tracking signal from the enemy Mole disappeared and bombers report an explosion. But the two were in different place outside the colony and the bombers weren't the cause of the explosion. They were following the Mole signal which had been going in an erratic formation almost since the bombings had begun." Rob nodded to Daniels as he absorbed all of the information and looked over the sensor data. While keeping his eyes on the sensor data, Rob replied to the officer, "Our bombers have been following a decoy."

Daniels looked confused at this. Saying as much by asking how. "I don't know. But they figured something out." Rob said and walked over to Jacob with the sensor data in hand.

Jacob looked up at the sounds of the close footsteps approaching and saw Rob with something in his hands. Looking back to his daughter as she still lay in her tears which had made her pass out mere moments ago.

Rob stopped in front of him. "Jacob, I need your help with this. They used the Mole as a decoy but we don't know how or what they're using. Cartwright could be at our door soon and we won't know."

Jacob didn't reply to him. Putting his arm on Jacob's should, Rob knelt down, face to face with Jacob he pleaded to his friend.

"Jacob. I know you're hurting right now. You've lost one son and another has gone AWOL. Your wife and son in law are who knows where doing we don't know what, and you're breaking. But you can't break. We need you at your best. I can help with technical and strategic assistance but you know every piece of technology out here. You made almost all of it. Please pull yourself together man!"

Jacob just stared at him another minute, then said. "How can I help anyone? I can barely stand myself. I never thought about how much losing my children would hurt me."

Rob had to fire Jacob up somehow. "Jacob, if you don't pull yourself back together you may lose Jack next or Melissa. You need to support Jack and protect Melissa. If you can't do that then, then, Dustin's sacrifice WAS for nothing!"

Jacob looked at Rob. Focusing, working to clear his head. Rob's outburst had awoken Melissa who turned and looked to him. She tapped her father's shoulder. When he looked down to her, she nodded. She agreed with Rob. Jacob agreed with Rob.

He stood up and asked, "What's the situation?"

Rob smiled briefly at his friend being back and brought up the screen again with the sensor data. "The Mole was a decoy but we don't know what they could be using to evade us," Rob replied.

Jacob examined it a moment and then put in some new searches for the sensors. Signals to look for. After no results Jacob pointed to a point on the data screen and said, "There's only one person in the Mole. It is a decoy. They must have found the EV suits."

Not feeling comforted by this Rob asked, "But if it's just EV suits we should be able to locate them based on their tech and heat signatures."

Jacob shook his head slightly. "Not these suits. Joe had me make him some special stealth EV suits a couple months back. I was doing them all on my own so no one but he and I knew of them. He took all four of them on the mission with him. They're double layered Graphene with outer camouflage and low powered internal systems. The way it works is its bullet proof, impact proof say for a large explosion. The suit uses wind energy from Mars' wind or Solar winds depending on the environment to power the cloaking, internal sensors, and oxygen recycling systems. The suit makes its wearers untraceable. Even hides their body heat and biochip signal. The ultimate in infiltration. The idiot should have used that to rescue Dustin though it was bulky and you could see it if you were looking at it so it may not have been feasible to use. Long story short, we won't find them looking for them." Rob was dumbstruck.

"Then how are we supposed to find them?!" he exclaimed.

"Well, they had to get to the surface somehow. Lieutenant Kabul, please look back on the sensors over the last few hours for signs of a hand drill in the surface."

Lieutenant Javier Kabul nodded from his station and began searching for the unique power signature in the logs, turning to communications, Jacob continued his roll. "Lieutenant Daniels, have you managed to get thru to Jack?"

Shaking his head Lieutenant Jon Daniels answered no. Wiping his face with his hands, Jacob stepped over to his station again and began working to get to his last son.

CHAPTER 21

They had made it. Capperman looked to his men and held a thumbs up. He could see the outer wall to Frontier Colony and by his sensors it was only 4.3 kilometers away. They'd be there in less than an hour. The suits that Capperman found in the Mole were the best, he had reviewed a manual installed on the faceplate monitor once he had suit up and activated the systems. Apparently these suits were prototype stealth suits.

As long as they were in these, no one could see or hurt them. Though he knew he'd be visible from someone standing right in front of him, and vulnerable to a bomb. But that was trivial so long as no one found them.

The only time he had been worried was when they had to blast their way to the surface. The suits had been running low on power and oxygen in the tunnel they were digging through so they couldn't wait the time it would take to finish drilling.

On a desolate surface where the enemy was looking for them, an explosion would just scream, "Here I am!" But luckily, Jing had them so far off that they didn't get to the explosion until after the team had gotten a good distance from the hole. While he was told these suits could evade a direct scan, Capperman didn't want to push his luck.

Capperman stopped suddenly, the others stopping right on his heel. His sensors had detected movement ahead. Zooming in to get a closer look, Capperman saw robots walking along the outer rim of the colony. Security Robots, he should have expected them to deploy Secbots, as they had been nicknamed decades ago.

Robots weren't used in a whole lot of places on Earth. They were considered Job killers when people needed work. But in these hostile climates, Robots were essential for progress to continue with limited cost of life. AIs were minimized to prevent all of those doomsday scenarios people had imagined a century earlier. Always had two people controlling and monitoring the bots from a safe and secure area.

Looking to his team, Capperman issued his new orders, "We need to split up, those Secbots won't see us if we can sneak around individually. If they do look at us from within 20 meters, they will spot us with those organic eyes of theirs. So keep your eyes peeled."

Zooming in and searching for an air lock on the outer wall, Capperman highlighted its position and sent the coordinates to his team members. "We'll meet at that air lock. Whoever gets there first needs to cover us in case some-one gets sighted. Second person to arrive will begin a clean breach. Remember, no bombs or shooting if you can help it. We don't want to draw attention to ourselves." Taking an extra moment to stare at McAllen. The cocky genius felt the hard stare of his superior through these impervious suits and knew to act the head on his shoulders for this mission.

The group of hardcore soldiers split with 30 meters between each person as they snuck into a field of hostile robots with orders to kill on sight. Each member knowing full well that even if they were to survive an encounter it would alert the Colonial militia to their location. McAllister had been excited this whole trip.

He had been just a soldier, a grunt until he fed Jensan to those sick inter-rogators. When he gave her to them, he didn't think they'd dice her up alive and then kill her. He just wanted to scare her. But it got him a promotion to Colonel Capperman's team and now he was looking for a way to get around those three eyed Secbots. The design of the Martian Secbot series was installed in the suit's memory.

After examining it, Capperman had told them all how to get around the crazy looking robots undetected. It was definitely easier said than done. With three eyes and sensors, they had to wait for a sand storm to come and cloud their vision. Checking the local conditions though, they knew one would be coming soon. McAllister was standing about 30 kilometers from his nearest sentry when the ground started rumbling. There weren't supposed to be earthquakes on Mars. Just then he noticed the ground starting to break not far from him.

Deciding he had no other choice but to make a run for it during the commotion. McAllister bolted towards the colony. Just behind him, the Mole popped up from beneath the ground. The Secbots all noticed the large drilling vehicle with no trouble and began rolling straight towards it, and McAllister.

Seeing the Secbots heading straight for him, McAllister was praying that this suit would do its Job. His suit suddenly announced incoming aircraft. Alarms began blaring alerting him to an incoming bomb.

Several bombs later, there was no sign of McAllister. Scrap metal all over the area showed what was left of the Mole and three Secbots that had been almost on top of McAllister and the Mole. Capperman looked on from the airlock. He had just reached it. When Jing arrived and created the distraction, Capperman ordered the team to move. That idiot Jing though had not only screwed herself and nearly the mission when she arrived in the Mole. But thanks to her recklessness McAllister had been caught in the crossfire and blown up.

Four people was a hard enough team to do what they had to do, but three now, now it would be damn near impossible, he thought.

McAllen got the airlock open and after entering, Capperman noticed a Secbot was turning, if they didn't reseal the airlock, they'd all be caught. Slamming the door shut nearly on himself. Capperman wasn't sure if they were seen or not but didn't want to wait around to find out.

The team walked down a corridor leading deeper into the colony. They kept their suits on to evade the cameras and sensors in the colony. Using an inferred sensor on the helmet, Farmer kept an eye out for anyone approaching while McAllen used his helmet to follow a map of the colony. They needed to find a security office and visual feed monitor.

From what the Lunar MI base had told them all those months ago, there was a center not far from this air lock that they could access both from. If it hadn't been moved though. This area was under construction for colony expansion so they had a security station to ensure no breaches in the colony.

The construction site, Capperman had noticed was a few clicks from where they had been. They began at the far wall using construction bots to build the foundation. Though Capperman did notice that there should have been someone around here by now. The construction bots hadn't been active so construction was at a halt for some reason. Capperman suspected it was because of the impending attack by Hawkeye Battalion.

Locating the security room, McAllen opened the door, Capperman and Farmer knocked out the guards using the stolen rifles to incapacitate the guards and avoid setting off alarms. Once the room was cleared, McAllan proceeded to hack into the main security system for the colony. Setting the internal feeds to a repeating loop, McAllan removed his helmet and gloves. Capperman went to secure the room and check the monitors for anyone else in the surrounding corridors. While Farmer restrained the unconscious guards and locked them up in a temporary cell adjacent to the security office.

After a few minutes, Capperman had come to the conclusion that there was no one else within the immediate vicinity of this station but that this station was monitoring the Secbots until the attack. After the bombers had left, the office had transferred control to the main base. Capperman had studied the layout of the colony and knew that this was a vast colony with open fields for farming, buildings similar to those on Earth and that it had been built around a canyon to allow for buildings built into the Martian walls.

The Military base was located on the far side of the colony, across a bridge and some farms on the other side of the canyon. The colony had a few mines for various resources forms of metal and ice. Getting to the base would be hard but they may be able to get to a mine. Controlling the ice mine could be key. It was the colony's main source of water and oxygen. There were some backup and storage units in the different levels of the system. Each section had been built capable of independent life support systems.

McAllan managed to lock up a frequency on the comms and secure it for a transmission to Mars Max. As Capperman stood by a monitor, his leader and friend appeared with a smile.

"I see you've made it to the Colony Colonel. Well done. Though it does seem that you lost your way back." He must have heard about the Mole getting bombed, though Capperman.

Nodding, Capperman replied to his CO's unasked question. "They were tracking the Mole so we went on foot. Jing had joined us and we left her in the Mole. She popped up just behind McAllister right in front of the Colony and a squad of Secbots. Thanks to that idiot, we lost a good man and almost got caught entering the city."

With a column stare as he listened to the report. Eric Cartwright took a moment to think, then asked, "Where are you currently?"

"In a security office along the entrance to where we came in. We're monitoring the corridors and inner entrances from here."

"I see," he said, nodding some more, and then suddenly his head motions stopped. "Get out of that area as soon as we finish this call. We haven't gotten this far by being sloppy. They will send a squad to check your area sooner or later and when that happens, I want you far away. McAllen, what's the approximate distance between security offices?"

Taking a moment to look at the colony map and utilizing a closed network search, McAllen found the answer the inquiry efficiently. Looking up to his CO, he replied, "There's an office near each airlock along the outer corridors. After we leave the outer corridors there is one every kilo in each direction. But those would be more crowded as they serve the masses."

Capperman cut him off with a shake of his head. "No, I have to disagree. They have evacuated the civilians, wherever the civilians are is where the bulk of their security will be. Each office will probably have ten men tops but few if any civilians. Though I would suggest we use civilian clothes and transport to get around more freely than in these. But we won't be leaving these suits behind, they are much too valuable to us."

Nodding with his hands to his mouth, an annoying habit of his when he listened to people stating, what to him, was the obvious. Cartwright approved the plan and told his top operatives that he was ready when they were, but was getting impatient.

* * *

Closing the channel, he hadn't told Capperman the unfortunate news. Just as Captain Ferguson's interrogation had begun, Cartwright had been interrupted with news that Dustin Fallok had shot himself. Suicide, obviously, which meant he was about to break. The idiot guards who allowed it to happen had been dealt with harshly, once Cartwright had finished reviewing the evidence.

Showing the video to Joseph Ferguson had had the opposite effect though that he had hoped. They thought that once Ferguson had seen the footage of the young man shooting himself, he would open up. Stupid mistake for everyone, if anything it only made Ferguson hold up even more. In the end, they got nothing useful out of him except good footage. He had a talk with Rashar about not killing everyone so quickly. 12 hours of interrogation is good, especially if you can keep them coherent, but killing them within six hours could not be tolerated.

Equally annoying was how hard it is to obtain truth serums. Chemicals were tightly controlled on Earth and nearly impossible to find in the regions Cartwright was serving in. Mars was even stricter with chemicals produced only in certain labs and not allowed to leave those labs without the highest security and even then it was tracked constantly. The medical ward at Mars Max had only the basics, anything serious would come from Frontier on a case by case basis, perhaps to prevent what Cartwright wanted.

Cartwright took comfort in the notion that soon, Frontier would fall with little bloodshed thanks to Joseph Ferguson.

CHAPTER 22

F rom comms, Lieutenant Daniels heard the confirmation and relayed it to the others. The enemy Mole had been destroyed and they found evidence of at least two bodies and ruble from three Secbots.

"I want a two teams sent to the nearest airlock. Send one team out to give us visual confirmation of all corpse. There should be four DNA/strands there. Second team needs to confirm that the airlock hasn't been breached and if so, locate the intruders." Commander Lee ordered from the center. She had arrive as part of plan B. Daniels entered the commands and while he got team 374, 375 had not replied. Twice more he tried to no success. Lee ordered 376 to inspect the security office at airlock 375. It appeared that they did breach and jump the security team. Once there's proof, Plan B enters stage 2.

Melissa had stepped back from the situation, after hearing about Dustin, she hadn't recovered. Equally, due to his hesitation, Jacob had also stepped back, referring to Commander Lee upon her arrival. He was still trying to get thru to Jack over the comms and having no success. He had learned faster than Jacob thought when he was growing up.

Kujai from sensors called out, "Lt. Fallok and Commander LeJoines have arrived at Mars Max and have initiated their bombardment. Enemy fighters have engaged, our men are outnumbered 2-1." Lee cursed for a moment, then asked Kujai where Captain Jung was. "Captain Jung dispatch Bomber Squad 2 in pursuit of the Lieutenant and Commander, currently they are two minutes behind. Bomber squad one headed towards the battle only moments ago upon being cleared after the enemy Mole was destroyed. Squad 2 had to come from Red Colony though hence their lapse." Kujai added before Lee could ask why Squad 2 had taken so long. Just because Mars Max was closest to Frontier didn't justify to the other colonies why they should have their air support taken. Seconds later, the sensors showed the aircraft above Mars Max shooting at each other. The firefight for Mars Max had begun.

At another station, Private Fo was monitoring internal sensors for the colony, trying to hunt down the intruders and communicating with the various security teams in the East quadrant of Frontier Colony. According to the freed security operatives, there were three intruders. They had stolen civilian attire and one of the guards' cars. After getting the information, Fo had put a system wide alert for three individuals in Jeans, a red button down, Plaid button down, and a black, red, and green Martian Manhunter t-shirt driving an '04 Toyota Jetstream, blue. License 3L44T8.

Normally, this would get instant hits across the board, but with most of the colony underground, the only people who would see would be security anyways. Though he wondered how hard would it be to notice a blue Jetstream in a sea of military vehicles. Getting an idea from this to search for the vehicle via its internal GPS chip brought the car up in front of the Boeing engine labs. Fo immediately alerted the nearby security teams to converge on the building. After issuing his verbal report to Commander Lee, Fo continued monitoring the situation, he couldn't get a biosign reading from the building, so either no one was there or they were masking their life signs somehow. Based upon what Mr. Fallok had told him, he wasn't surprised by that.

Commander Lee, Jacob Fallok, Rob Bellington, and Lieutenant Kujai were watching the fire fight above Mars Max. Jack and Tyler were definitely living up to their reputations and quickly overturning the odds in their favor. Their backup was still one minute out and the cargo ships at Mars Max were trying to evacuate the base. Jacob was beginning to feel optimistic that this whole thing may end in this battle.

The security teams arrived at the vehicle to find it empty, the building was still sealed shut with no sign of entry. The vehicle had been dumped and by the heat of the engine the team leader had determined that they were ten minutes behind, though Fo had corrected that the vehicle had been stationary for 15 minutes. That left a huge lead for the intruders to have infiltrated the vast and empty colony built for over a quarter of a million people.

"Captain Jung confirms cargo ships and escorts leaving Martian atmosphere." Daniels announced from Comms. "Reports that enemy group is regrouping with enemy forces holding in space. Jung requests permission to pursue." A moment later, before Lee could say anything, Daniels continued, "General Decker has green light for Captain Jung attack. Space battle is a go."

Kujai announced his verbal report from Mars Max, "Bombers have arrived, Mars Max under siege by friendly forces, all crafts not in air are grounded or disabled. Captain Jung has sent transport craft to Mars Max to confront ground forces. Bombers are staying put, Lieutenant Fallok and Commander LeJoines have agreed to wait for Jung's commandos before setting down."

There were cheers among the soldiers and scientists rallied in the Command Center, though there was still a space battle starting and a rigorous manhunt going on. Fo had dispatched all available teams in the quadrant to find the intruders and a barrier had been set up to lockout that quadrant from the rest of the colony. Though anyone with a detailed map and time to study it, may be able to find one or two ways through, Fo had set up teams in those weak sections. Though those teams hadn't gotten to their destinations yet so right now, he was praying for luck.

CHAPTER 23

McAllan gave out a yelp as he received a slight shock from the wire he was rerouting. "There, all done sir."

Capperman smiled, they had eluded the security teams so far and found a tech lab they were able to sneak into to get access to the colony's communications. Hacking into the emergency override system, they will get onto every monitor, Holodisplay, and headset monitor in the colony.

Before switching it on, McAllen had made sure it wouldn't be tracked to this room and they had sealed the door from the inside. Though Farmer was keeping a gun on the door just in case. Opening a private channel to Mars Max, Cartwright pickup up after a moment and a transfer.

"About time John! We're being attacked here!" Capperman was taken aback, they didn't think they'd attack yet. Capperman asked the obvious question of how they were faring. "How do you think we're doing? I sent what ships could get off the ground up to space, but reports show there is a battle starting up there too. Ground forces are inbound here. We need to transmit the recording and get this to stop." Capperman nodded and gave the okay to McAllen.

McAllen activated the emergency program and Cartwright began transmitting his recording, all over the colony everyone would see this.

The image of Eric Cartwright in full military dress appeared on screen. *"People of Frontier Colony, I am General Eric Cartwright of the New United Earth Force. We have a simple goal in mind, to police humanity and the Earth to and protect humanity from itself. Our first enemy however has been Frontier Colony. Now, we aren't arbitrarily attacking everyone. Everyone has a choice, Join us, Don't Join us, or think about it. Though to give you some incentive, here is one of those who joined us."*

A man and woman appeared in front of the screen, she was tall, brunette, white, piercing green eyes, and quite beautiful. He was equally tall, handsome, of a darker complexion, short dark hair and bright brown eyes. They said their names, occupations, and how happy they've been since joining the New United Earth Force. Abruptly, Cartwright cut back to him.

He then continued, *"However, if you choose not to join us, behold that fate."*

The camera cut to a dark room, light shown only on one individual, He was partially mutilated and screaming in agony. He didn't know there was a camera showing him, nor would he probably care.

"State your name and rank!" a voice in the shadows called.

The broken man replied with almost no defiance left, *"Captain Joseph Ferguson."*

The voice from the shadows called out, *"Where are you stationed!"*

"Frontier Colony Mars Defense Force, Commander."

"What happened to your godson, Dustin Fallok?"

"He killed himself after you beheaded two women trying to get him to talk. He was the brave one, I only wish I was as strong."

"Thank you Captain Ferguson, your pain is almost at an end." A man came out of the shadows and sawed off another joint. Every monitor, display, and speaker in Frontier Colony reverberated with the ear splitting scream as joint after joint was sawed off of Joseph Ferguson. Between screams he begged them to kill him. After 15 minutes of this broadcast, the monster on the screen fulfilled Joseph's pleas and removed his head. Letting the head fall from its shoulders, the head of Joseph Ferguson rolled conveniently enough, straight to the camera, showing his horrible terror immobilized at death, eyes open in horror.

The screen cut back to Cartwright, he smiled and shook his head slowly. *"Tsk, tsk, tsk, that was sad to watch, all he had to do was pledge loyalty to our cause and tell us what we wanted to know. Now it's too late. You must live with your choices as he and so many others have. So Frontier Colony, you have three hours to announce loyalty to me, or die. I'll be seeing you soon, either way."* With one last cut to Joseph's head, the screen tuned out.

All over the colony, there were people screaming in terror, crying, vomiting. The emergency shelters were on the verge of mass hysteria following the death of their chief protector and the beloved son of one of the founding fathers of Frontier. The people didn't know what to do. Their peaceful and fruitful lives had just been thrown asunder. They were given a choice of live under a military dictator or die a gruesome and painful death. Nothing else had been forthcoming after more than five minutes. Though how could the people blame them. No one was prepared for that. No one could prepare for that.

Back in the Command Center, the room was stunned. The transmission had jammed all signals in and out so they couldn't keep tabs on the battle of Mars Max or in orbit. But after watching the gruesome death of Joe and hearing confirmation of Dustin's suicide. Jacob was beyond distraught. He was feeling a kind of hatred he had never felt before. He wanted to ring Eric Cartwright's neck in his hands until the monster breathed no more. Jacob Fallok, the ever pragmatic, life loving, optimistic, supporting man; was out for blood.

After a few minutes of calming himself, Jacob put in a call to Mayor Graleen who effectively placed Jacob in charge of the situation and went into hiding with the CEOs, Ambassadors, chief scientists, and bureaucrats at the secure shelter in Memory Alpha. After that, Jacob reactivated the emergency channel, though allowing the military to continue use of its stations and communications. Showing himself to all of Frontier Colony and anyone within Martian space listening, Jacob began to fight back.

"Frontier Colony, My friends, my family, colleagues, and fellow humans. We are at war. We did not choose this war, nor can we take a neutral stance in this war. Its fight or die and so far, we are losing. They shed the first blood. Hundreds of people have already died in this war including my eldest son, my brother and our chief protector, and as we speak, my wife and son in law are fighting them underground, my other son is fighting them at their base, and our space forces are battling them in orbit. We have not taken this lying down.

"They are few, they are strangers to this place. This is our home and we will defend our home from anyone who dares to take it from us. We need anyone willing to help, this is what we have been preparing for so many months and now the time has come. Join me my brothers and sisters of Frontier Colony! Help me push these invaders from our home before your children, brothers, sisters, husbands, or wives become victims and many others have. Anyone willing to join please speak to your area reps. We will be victorious as we stand united. Godspeed."

With fire in his eyes, Jacob closed the channel. Commander Lee was looking at him she, "Your orders sir?" It was time for decisive action.

"Have anyone who volunteers to be crowd control. If we can get civilians to police themselves in the shelters, we can mobilize all of our forces on the man hunt for the intruders. I want them found before Cartwright can make another move." Lee seemed inquisitive.

"Sir, isn't Cartwright under siege at Mars Max at the moment?"

Jacob shook his head. "I doubt it. I'm willing to bet he's on a cargo vessel that escaped Mars Max. What was the status of the orbital battle?"

Kujai turned to Jacob. "Equally matched battle, though two cargo ships left the battle heading here. All forces are either at Mars Max or in orbit. A single fighter left the fight to pursuit the ships but at least one will get to Frontier and be able to touch down."

"Have we sent troops to intercept once it lands?" Lee nodded to Jacob. Soon as she heard, she had dispatched five squads of fifteen men to the spaceport to work with port security and be waiting where ever they touch down. Though she had noticed a weakness in the system and felt she needed to point it out.

"Jacob, I need to point out a flaw here." Seeming intrigued he encouraged her to continue. "We've mobilized all forces to find the intruders, intercept the cargo ship, safe guard the civilians, and sent off all air craft to two battles. We moved our command center to this bunker deep below your house in the center of the colony, but we've left a skeleton crew at our military base. There's virtually no one there to defend it should it come under attack or to intercept should the Hawkeyes attempt to land there."

Putting his right hand to his chin and stroking the short beard that had been growing over the last week, Jacob was generally dumb struck by this revelation. He hadn't even thought about how many people he had stripped from the base.

Turning to Private Fo at internal sensors, "Private Fo, pull up all ground forces I wanna know how many and where."

Nodding to the man in charge, Fo brought up a hologram of the colony with blue lines showing skeletal structures and green dots showing military forces, blue dots showing police forces, grey showing civilians. At the side of the display, another display showed a graph of how many of each dot in the section being viewed.

After a couple minutes skimming through the whole colony, Jacob determined each quadrant had roughly 500 military and police forces and the space port had 700 thanks to the increased forces Lee had just sent, and its own security teams. Though the base only had 75 soldiers.

"Wow, I can't believe we took so many forces away from the base and that with 2000 armed forces we can't find three people."

Lee nodded in agreement and shame. These were her men, Frontier Colony's defense force was supposed to be the best thanks to the colony's wealth. But they couldn't find three strangers to the land.

"Lt. Daniels, send 100 men from each quadrant back to the base. That should even things out. Then scour every room in every quadrant. We need to find those intruders before they hack anymore systems. Try the heat scanners again. I doubt they're still in those suits and any hot spots the size of a body need to be checked against our forces. Any civilians should also be stopped and checked." Checking the scanners, once more, Fo didn't find anything.

But then on a hunch, he checked a different sensor. Airlock controls, and found something. "Sir! They're using airlocks! According to airlock records, after they entered through the initial one at 384, 15 minutes after conclusion of Cartwright's broadcast another airlock was accessed at 237. Ten minutes later, Airlock 198 was accessed, that brought them into the south quadrant. There was a civilian car driven southbound for 15 minutes with no biosigns in the car. Team 35 heading back to the military base found the car on the side of the road. It showed signs of remote driving but it could be a diversion." Jacob gave Fo a pat on the back.

"Good call Private. It could be a ruse but it could also be a reverse ruse. Keep an eye on airlock activity and have team 34 spread out and search from there all the way to the base. The Spaceport is in East Quadrant so we should be okay unless you find proof of access to East." Fo became a bit jittery.

"Um, sir. Only West Quadrant was closed off. If they got into South, they could very well be in East or North Quadrants by now." Jacob cursed at this.

"You're right of course. We should have sealed up all the sectors when we closed off West. We have enough teams between the base and spaceport though that we should find them." Fo being the ever pragmatic individual he was, felt he had to point out the obvious.

"Sir, beg your pardon, but our 2000 men sure haven't had any luck finding them so far, and it's been five hours. We kinda suck at manhunts it seems." Commander Lee was stunned by this outburst, as was everyone within earshot. Lee, quickly recovering got up into Fo's face.

"That was out of line Private! Your attitude is out of line and Mr. Fallok your superior and had not given you permission to speak freely. Am I understood?"

Fo took his reprimand and nodded to his commanding officer, then apologized to Jacob. But Jacob didn't seem mad. "No need to apologize. You're right."

Lee did a double take blink at this, as did Fo. "You're right, Private. We've never had to do a manhunt for ghosts. These three are amazing at using my technology to hide from us. They avoid heat scanners, bio scanners, they don't have personnel chips like the rest of us. Using remote cars, a trick nearly a century old but still effective. How do we..."

Jacob slapped a hand to his face. "Why didn't I think of it before? The emergency transponder. Of Course!" Everyone around him was clearly confused at Jacob's rant. None of them new what he was talking about, and it showed. "The stealth suits I built have an emergency transponder," he explained.

"In case the wearers were in need of assistance, they could activate the emergency transponders. On the flip side, in case of loss of life or local trouble, the transponder would automatically activate in the case of the former, or I could remotely activate the transponder. But they would know as soon as I do. So they will do one of two things when I activate it. Either loose the suits, at which point we can get a bio and heat sig on them, or try and disable it. Though it'll take at least one of them a good couple minutes to figure out how to shut it down."

Typing in a frequency, Jacob turned to Fo, as soon as I activate it, look for this signal. You may only have 30 seconds so look hard. Mel! Come here please I need you!" Jacob yelled across the room to his daughter who promptly stood up and sped over to her father. "Assist Private Fo while he's looking for the transponder signal, I want you searching for bio and heat signatures. If you find both nearly on top of each other. Keep track of those life signs."

Both young adults nodded and got to work searching. Jacob went to his personal terminal and brought up the transponder program. "Okay, people, I'm activating the transponders in."

As he began a countdown to activation, he typed in the codes. Everything needed to be timed perfectly. They were running out of time and options.

"Three, two, one." He hit the activate button. "Active. Find those signals."

The seconds rolled by slowly. Jacob had Lee watching the other battles and cargo ships while he focused on the manhunt. Moments later, Fo called out, "I've got a signal sir!"

Melissa picked it up as well. "Three bio signs emerging slowly on that spot! Tracking!" Said an excited Melissa. Jacob then asked where they are. "East Quadrant, oh no," Melissa said, then Fo took over.

"Sir, they're inside spaceport control room," Fo said, before being told he began dispatching teams to the control room. "I've already dispatched teams, sir, but how could they get so deep?"

"They did their homework and caught us with our pants down. Which won't happen again." Jacob said with determination. "How long till the nearest team arrives?"

"One minute, sir."

"Mel, you still have eyes on their bio signs?"

"Yes, Daddy, they won't get away again."

"Good." Turning to Lee for a moment, Jacob asked, "Status on cargo vessels?"

"Lead Cargo vessel steered towards our base as we suspected it may. Second on is still heading for spaceport. Fighter is heading to first one," she said.

"No, have him maintain pursuit of the second one. He's closer to it, and since the intruders are at the spaceport. The first is clearly a decoy meant to divert the fighter."

"But what if that is the diversion? The spaceport has more security at the moment."

"Wondering if the decoy is a decoy to do what it shouldn't. That's second guessing, we have one fighter and two enemy vessels in opposite directions. The fighter is closer to one, it should continue pursuit of that one. We don't have time for second guessing."

Lee nodded to his words of wisdom and enacted the orders. Turning back to the internal situation, Jacob asked for a status report.

"Teams are in pursuit. The intruders fled soon as they stripped the suits off. I have maintained eyes on them and Private Fo has kept the teams in pursuit. Though they are good. Almost like they can see the teams coming from three corridors away." Melissa reported.

"Can we get cameras on them? They could be scanning corridors for biosigns to determine where to move."

"Working now," Fo said. A moment later, an image appeared showing the three intruders two with guns in hand and another with a scanner. Jacob went to his console and tapped in a few commands with authorization. Melissa and Fo were still focusing on the video feed to see what they could discern from their enemy. A moment later, the image died. "Daddy!" Melissa called out, "We just lost the feed!" Jacob came over.

"Show us the bio signs again. I killed the feed." Melissa looked curiously at her father and asked why he would do that. "I sent a miniature EM Burst in that corridor. Disabling all of their gadgets as well as ours. Say for the bio signs from satellite. Lights are also disabled. How soon till a team arrives?"

Looking at the display, Fo replied seconds. But as soon as the readings showed the presence of new life signs in the corridor, they began disappearing. In less than two minutes, ten lives were gone and the three intruders were still standing. Sensors didn't show a single shot fired either.

The colonists had finally learned the capabilities of their intruders and it was worse than expected. They didn't need gadgets to see or guns to kill and they were using guerilla warfare on the enemy's home turf. Now Jacob knew what they'd been up to on the six month trip to Mars, extensive planning of every detail. While little was known about the battalion and its people, there was trilobites of information on Frontier colony and its personnel. Jacob's attention was then caught by a sound from Commander Lee. Turning to her, he asked what happened.

"As the fighter approached the second cargo ship, it sent out a missile. We didn't know it was an armed transport. The ships manifest showed botanical and metallurgical equipment. We lost the fighter and both ships are landing at both locations.

The Hawkeyes have come for us."

Walking to the loading dock of the cargo ship Jackson, Eric Cartwright could hear the sound of laser fire ringing thru the corridors. They had landed and the defense forces were on them before the engines could finish turning off. Every entrance was a fire fight. Cartwright was heading to the large cargo dock to exit, why let them pick him off one at a time at one of the airlock exits after all.

Looking at his watch, everything was running on schedule, to the minute. Impressing even himself with how well his plans had worked so far. This was after all, the first time the MDF had an actual war to fight. Just as he had entered the battle at the open cargo dock, his men were outnumbered and starting to loose.

A MDF soldier saw Eric and yelled out, "Eric Cartwright, surrender your forces. You are outnumbered and out gunned."

Nodding to the soldier with a dark and arrogant smile, Cartwright raised his arms in the air. "You're a brave man standing up to me like that. Would you like to join us in our cause?" Cartwright said, slowly, while making such strong eye contact at his enemy.

The man started sweating profusely as he replied, "Join you? I'm arresting you! Now come quietly!" The heightened anxiety in his voice was loud and clear. Eric was nervous only because an unstable man was pointing a gun straight at him. But he dare not show an inkling of anything but arrogance and determination.

Though he could already see those behind the Defense Force soldiers. "I'm sorry you won't be around long enough to see the errors you have made today."

As the soldier and his men began turning to each other in confusion, they each began dropping to the floor as Cartwright's reinforcements arrived.

Flanking the Defense Force soldiers, John Capperman and his team arrived just in time to help Cartwright. Looking at his watch again, Cartwright smiled and walked across the loading dock, now with only his forces standing, he approached Capperman and gave his number one man a hug. "Exactly on time my friend." Capperman smiled and with a curt nod, he turned to everyone else and began issuing orders.

All hands were told to be as far from the ship after 30 minutes from landing as possible. So many were running from the ship but the slower one got stuck in fire fights with colonial forces. Cartwright and his teams from the loading dock were halfway across the landing field when the cargo ship exploded, taking half of the landing field with it and further crippling Frontier Colony of some 200 soldiers that were too close to the ship and opening in the dome. Emergency barriers came in to seal that half before more got sucked out. Cartwright knew he had most likely just lost half of his crew from the ship, the weaker part, and so he paid it no mind.

Turning to his most loyal and trusted friend, Cartwright asked, "How did your diversionary tactics work?"

Capperman, putting on that hideous smile he had thanks to facial scars replied, "We'll be in the clear well out of this area provided that idiot soldier didn't let them know you were here. Their sensors should think you were on the other ship at the base. But these fools are learning, as we made our way here, they kept getting closer to us. Almost caught us twice even and I'm almost positive that they're tracking us now."

Cartwright was getting angry from this news. He knew it would happen eventually, but he didn't like the idea of being tracked so soon, and said as much. "General, the last time they tried something, they blocked us in a corridor, used a micro EM burst and sent 20 men in the corridor to apprehend us. They know we were the only ones who left alive, but the main thing is, they know we are three and have therefore been sending out groups of five to make it easier to find us by merely looking for a group of three on the bio sensors. Though I do have a plan sir. Since we can now be a group of five, we ambush a group and steal their trackers and uniforms."

Looking at Capperman, Cartwright wanted to smack him for such a simple stupid idea. But perhaps, that was the genius of it. Stupid, simple plans work because of the simplicity of it. And when your enemy thinks you are doing complicated things, they won't look for the simple ones.

"Okay, John, we'll do it. We need to get to their operations controls. Do we know where it is yet since they moved it?"

Capperman shook his head in the negative and replied, "They have so many levels both above and below the surface, plus in the canyon, that we haven't been able to track the source of communications and other activities. And when we interrogated some of the soldiers on our way here, none of them could tell us. The location is apparently Alpha Level security. Whoever is in charge is keeping anyone with that knowledge close by and away from us."

Thinking a moment, Cartwright came up with his next phase. "If Fallok is keeping his top people near him, we're screwed. But I think that would be too many people. I imagine there has to be someone with Alpha level in each shelter the people are hiding in. We need to get to a shelter."

CHAPTER 25

"They blew their own ship up?!" Lee asked in shock at the news. Melissa confirmed it and furthered the news, "We lost 176 military transponders in the blast and 47 during the combat beforehand. Unsure how many enemy troops were killed in the fighting and blast, but we did track four large groups heading away at high speeds prior to the blast. The blast also tore up four of our six commercial landing pads in that section of the space port." Fo had been tracking the situation at the base and gave his report.

"News on the second ship is slightly better. Our forces were able to breach the enemy ships early enough to find and disable the self-destruct. Still heavy casualties though. 87 transponders lost. Unknown number of injuries. Due to our resistance at killing, we have captured 124 enemy soldiers from the ship, though an unknown number did escape. Based on calculations at the maximum number of people to safely fit in the ship. There couldn't be more than 210 people. But that is for a short trip like the one they took and with minimal cargo since the majority of the people would be in the cargo hold." Jacob nodded to Fo in acknowledgement of the calculation.

Based on the information received, those numbers made sense. Though they hadn't counted on 420 highly trained soldiers and ex-criminals landing simultaneously and over powering nearly 1000 defense force soldiers. It was daunting just how bad the MDF was doing in this war. They had lost every battle so far except for the retaking of Mars Maximum that Jack had led.

From the reports received, Mars Max was back in the colony's possession. Jack's forces were in the process of freeing the surviving guards and researchers, recovering Dustin and Joe's bodies as well as those of Joe's Black Op team to bring back for burial. With all surviving enemy soldiers imprisoned Jack had begun sending people back to Frontier Colony to help against the invaders. But those reinforcements wouldn't arrive for two hours.

"Send all forces to the spaceport and base. We can't let the Hawkeyes get any further in our home," Jacob ordered.

The battle in space had been more equal than anticipated. Both sides had heavy losses. But one thing Jacob had now begun to suspect, is that the space forces were running with skeleton crews on the Hawkeye ships since the ground forces were so numerous. The space battle and retaking of Mars Max were both diversionary tactics to lower the forces defending Frontier Colony. And they had fallen for every single one of Cartwright's tricks. Jacob had to figure out Cartwright's next move and stop it before the whole colony fell to a ruthless force.

He began speaking aloud, hoping ideas might pour from others. "If you were an invading force, where would you go first?" he said. Melissa looked to him and replied. "Here."

"That's it!" he said, snapping his fingers. "They would come here, to the emergency command bunker since the other one was compromised by the capture of Joe. We have to assume that Dustin or Joe divulged the location of this bunker to the enemy, though I doubt it. They proved just how willing they were to put their lives before us. Let us not put their sacrifices to waste. Due to our equal distance from both the base and spaceport, we don't know where or when the attack may come from. Hence why it's imperative we find and follow if not stop all enemy troop movements. The biggest difference here is, they don't have a central command post to organize and adjust troop movements. We do."

Lieutenant Daniels requested Jacob's attention a moment later. Walking over to his communications man, Daniels began right away.

"Sir, I've gotten reports from South and East Quads of Hawkeyes ripping out military transponders from our people's flesh. Some are being killed, some aren't. But sir, I've tracked some of the reported transponders of those killed in action. They're still on the move."

Jacob's eyes widened. "They're trying to blend in and confuse our tracking methods. Private Fo!" Turning to one of the sensor monitors, he ordered, "Work with Daniels to track any transponders that we know are being used by the enemy. Mel, track any biosigns without transponders that are moving with those transponders."

With his newest orders being carried out, Jacob went to his own station. Lee was keeping him updated and was in charge of the other battles while he focused on the colony itself. Jacob was at his console thinking about Cartwright's actions. In his announcement, he had said he'd be here in three hours.

He arrived at the colony exactly on the mark. Exceptional planning and strategy. But why hadn't Cartwright just sent his undercover team straight here? He thought everyone in this business knew that a small team strategic and precise attack on an unsuspecting foe is more likely to succeed than a large troop movement. Unless he doesn't know where to send the team. He doesn't know where to go. And the only ones who know where to go are in the shelters. The one with Alpha security clearance in each Shelter. Jacob had to get them out, but he was unsure if communications were compromised. Airing on the side of caution, he chose not to send out a signal. Instead, deciding to send a team out.

"Lt. Gregory, please come here," Jacob called out to the head of the guards inside the bunker. When the man approached along with Commander Lee, Jacob gave out his orders.

"Lt. Take a four man team of your best men to each shelter, I want you to extract the Alpha Level people from the shelters and bring them here. Secretly give the Betas only the necessary information they need to maintain Shelter operations."

At his nod, Jacob handed over a manila envelope. "Here is a hard copy of the names of those you are extracting and their replacements. There is to be no digital copy of these names due to the potential for them to be hacked or leaked. These names are not to be announced over any communications system or even called out aloud. And do not refer to them as anything that can be used to identify them or their positions. Their safety as well as your own is at stake. Also in that folder is an underground map that links all of the shelters to each other so that you do not need to go to the surface. Lastly, these documents are made of a special synthetic composition, if a page gets one tear in it, even a small one, the inner layer's exposure to oxygen will cause the whole piece to crumble to ashes instantly. Should you be compromised, destroy all documents, at the same time, protect them. The colony is relying on you, Lieutenant Gregory."

The lieutenant nodded to Jacob and saluted his superiors before departing with folder in hand.

CHAPTER 26

Team assembled and departed in a convoy of three subterranean vehicles, Matt Gregory led his team to the first shelter on the detailed plan laid out by Jacob Fallok, this was closest to where reports showed the enemy advancing. Which meant they would have to stay a step ahead of the enemy at each shelter. The benefit of course being that they were using top secret tunnels below the shelters that few knew of. Second being that the enemy didn't know what they were up to, yet. One thing that everyone had figured out rather quickly was that the enemy knew them and their strategy better than the colonists did. Eric Cartwright had seemed to be a step ahead at every point; until now.

Cartwright may be able to find a few shelters, but he doesn't have the firepower to breach them. The tech know how though, he could breach if he can hack the code. It's because of this that the code was constantly rotating and very large and random. Using a combination of three languages and numbers, changing every two hours. But if the code is entered incorrectly it will begin randomizing a new code with different languages as well.

As they approached the shelter, someone was standing outside the sealed door. A guard by the looks of it. "Halt!" She said, "Who are you and how did you get here?" As she said this she raised her side arm to the security group.

Gregory slowly raised his hands as did his men. As he slowly approached her, his men stayed behind so as not to startle her. "I am Lieutenant Mathew Gregory, Jacob Fallok sent me here to check on the status of the shelters. The comms have become compromised requiring us to do personal checks on each shelter. These emergency tunnels are how we are going about our task underveil from the enemy to whom if you weren't aware, have invaded the colony in force and have our people are on the run, turning the surface into a battlefield.

The guard lowered her side arm. "If I can't use my radio, we're stuck here. To prevent me from letting someone in, I don't have the password, they have to open it from the inside."

Giving the guard a reassuring smile, Gregory patted the young girl, he could finally tell, on the shoulder. "Don't worry I will take care of it but could you please do me a favor and do a quick id scan for me Ms..."

"Landau, Shelly Landau. Okay, I guess that's understandable." As one of the other team members came to Shelly with a palm scanner, Gregory went up to the door to put the code in. 51م‌رحبا אמouit3, and watched the door open.

Leaving most of the group inside, Gregory walked into the shelter escorted by Shelly and two other men. The only information they were had to share was a photo with description of a thin, bald, black man. 3.2 meters tall, brown eyes, and he would be wearing dark blue jeans and a Frontiersman jersey as a fan of the colony's basketball team.

Once Shelly was shown the photo though, she knew exactly where to find him. Within ten minutes they were face to face with the target. In greeting, Gregory asked, "Please come with us sir and give your code work to your beta." Nodding to the soldier, the man stepped away for a few minutes and returned.

"Okay, I'm ready to go lieutenant." Turning around, Gregory and his team escorted their first guest back to the caravan. Once the shelter door was resealed, Shelly went back to her post. Until Gregory halted her. "I'm sorry Ms. Landau but you need to come with us as well. You have seen our forces and know what we are up to. I need to keep you with us. Think of it as you are your Alpha's body guard." Nodding to him, she conceded his point and went to sit next to her charge in the second van.

After the caravan of cars turned en route to the next pickup, Gregory turned to his second in command. "Already ahead of schedule, it'd be nice if this keeps up."

With a quizzical face, the other man asked, "You think this will get harder?" Gregory turned to his second and with a stare as though the man had two heads.

"Of course, so does Fallok. As soon as Cartwright gets into the colony and finds out what he is looking for isn't there, he'll go faster and though he'll be a step behind us for a few shelters, he'll catch up rather quickly. Unless we can get each one done in 20 minutes like we just did, we will get stuck in a confrontation."

Kim Je Lo looked at his superior and mentor and then stared on at the tunnel ahead and silently prayed for a peaceful and quick end to this mission as the caravan sped thru toward the second of 32 shelters.

CHAPTER 27

After only an hour of fighting, Mars Maximum was once more in the hands of its guards and the colonies. All escapees and remaining Hawkeyes had been captured with no casualties on their end, thanks to Dr. Bellington's new stun lasers. Unfortunately, the same could not be said on their end. Colonial forces had taken a lot of casualties as had the guards.

As soon as he was able to, Jack Fallok had sent anyone back to Frontier he could. But as leader of this battle, his place was here with his men. Tyler, try as Jack might, would not leave his side. The two were partners and Tyler would stay by Jack's side until the end of this conflict or the end of their lives.

He found the bodies of his brother and Joe and the other victims of from the interrogations. Holding his dead brother, Jack finally broke down. Tyler held him for long time until Jack could compose himself again. They were nearing their next goal of bringing their family home for burial.

CHAPTER 28

"Dad, Hawkeyes are approaching the first shelter!" Melissa Fallok exclaimed from her station.

Jacob was quickly by her side. "Has the trap been set?" he asked.

"Yes, but they haven't triggered yet, a little closer. The inhabitants are prepared to evacuate via the tunnels if they get thru the trap." Jacob's hardest thoughts went to the citizens in the shelters. He put them there to keep them safe, but he made them a target. A farm of fresh victims and recruits alike for Cartwright's hell bent army. Melissa snapped him out of his revelry, exclaiming, "Trap triggered!" Guns blazing, two buildings came down atop the enemy forces between them. Remaining forces began climbing over the debris with no thought to those underneath. As the enemy was mounting the new hill, defense force soldiers were picking them off like ducks in a shooting gallery. At the same time, more contingents of defense force soldiers were boxing in the Hawkeyes from behind. After 20 minutes of battle, the remaining Hawkeyes surrendered. The shelter was safe. The colony won a battle.

Back at the command center, there were celebratory cries with the turnout. But then an alarm went off. Yu's console jumped to another sector of the city. "Jacob! Shelter 23 has just been breached!" Shock all around. Jacob moved to Yu's side, looking at the readouts. Shelter 23 was 14 kilometers away from where the rest of Cartwright's forces were. Of course a large troop movement would be a diversion. Looking at the time and thinking where Lieutenant Gregory would be, hopefully, his team had finished in there but it would be close. Looking to Melissa he asked, "How many people are with Cartwright?"

"Nine, and all ten of them have DF bio chips."

"So, that's why we didn't see them, they were hiding right under our noses dressed as a contingent." Yu called out, "Jacob, I'm finding five other sets of ten near shelters. This was supposed to be a timed attack I believe." Horror now. Gregory couldn't have gotten to all of those shelters already. They needed DF forces there right away.

"Get any soldiers to each shelter as fast as possible!" That victory was too short lived, Jacob thought back to.

CHAPTER 29

W alking thru his sixth shelter, this Job had already begun becoming mostly redundant. Matt Gregory had only had a couple problems but other than that he was going very efficiently. Suddenly an alarm klaxon blared throughout the shelter. Followed quickly by a prerecorded announcement.

"Shelter doors compromised, evacuation plan Charlie initiated." The announcement would repeat three more times before ceasing. Timed to prevent the invaders from hearing it. The front entrance had three layers of doors to get through as a precaution and way to make time for evacuation. Though it was the same passcode for all three when entering, the leader on the inside had the capability to change the codes manually at each door to slow down the invaders further.

In an orderly fashion, people filled in lines to begin their exodus from the shelter into the back tunnels. Gregory and his men had to start wading through the crowds to get to the alpha, who as holder of the passcodes was trying to slow down the invaders. The Beta, in doing his part, was beginning the exodus at the head of the crowd.

After long minutes of wading thru the moving and panicked citizens, Gregory made it to the front control room where the Alpha and a skeleton crew were manning the doors and evacuation. "Ms. Dimitry, we have to leave!" Matt said from the door. The determined woman shook her head.

"No! If I can slow them down long enough to evacuate everyone, I mustn't give up!"

"Can't you just seal the doors?"

"They are sealed Mr. Greggory, its keeping them sealed that is the problem. They are hacking the system, in the time it takes me to put up a firewall, they break the previous one. If I stop or even slow down, they will be thru those doors in a minute!"

"Can't someone else take over for you?"

"Mr. Fallok's computer chose me for this site. I will defend my charges until they are all safe or die trying."

Matt turned to Kim, "Lieutenant Lo, assist with the evacuation. Radio me when everyone is thru. If we aren't at the door within five minutes of your radio, seal the door, weld it shut, and finish the mission."

With an abrupt salute, Lo said, "Yes, sir." Lo then took the rest of the men and left to help.

Turning back to Ms. Dimitry, Matt Gregory began assisting with the firewalls. "Thank you for your help Mr. Gregory. But you should know, you just sealed our fate." She said without missing a beat at her console.

"Oh?" said Matt, with a smile. "And how is that?"

Smiling back, she said, "No one has made it from here to the back door in less than seven minutes."

"Oh, I know. But we'll go down and take as many as we can with them."

"Do me one favor Matt."

"Name it."

"I saw the video of Captain Ferguson. If we are nearing capture, kill me."

"Sorry to be a downer, honey, but that was my orders."

Minutes later, the doors breached. As they stood in the control room awaiting the invaders, they kissed and while in the embrace, Matt stabbed his wife in the heart as quickly and painless as he could. He whispered, "I love you, dear" in her ear. Tears on both of their faces. He gently lowered her to the ground.

The doors to the control room blasted open just then. Matt turned to the enemy. "You're too late. She's dead. And so are you," he said as he dropped a grenade blowing the entire room away.

CHAPTER 30

Lo saw the control room blow just as he was getting the last of the civilians out of the shelter. He knew his mentor wasn't coming. This was his mission now. Turning and heading out of the shelter, the Beta sealed the door. "Time to finish Evac Plan Charlie," he said. The new civilian leader slowly nodded his head. Putting his new alpha clearance code into the door system, he finalized the plan and on the other side of the door, the shelter resealed the front doors and collapsed in on itself. "Lead your charges to the next shelter. We will alert them of your arrival." Lo got back in his lead car and the caravan went on to the next shelter.

* * *

In another part of the colony, Lieutenant Yu saw a light go out on his console. "Mr. Fallok! We've lost contact with Shelter 15!" Jacob was by the man's side in a heartbeat.

"Do we know what happened?"

"Pulling up a Shelter System report for 15 now." Looking over the report of the invasion and plan Charlie's enacting and completion. The two men at the console were flabbergasted. While yes, the plan worked out perfectly. It was Plan C because they didn't want it to get to that drastic of a situation. Jacob pulled up a casualty report. Just two deaths for the colony, 10 enemy. Though looking at the security footage for the two. It was hard to watch Mathew Gregory kill his wife per Jacob's orders and then himself, taking out ten enemy troops.

Jacob walked away from Yu's station. He had to step back for a minute. Review his actions. Because of his orders, a man just killed the love of his life and then himself. It was time for Jacob to stop hiding. He had to take down Cartwright now to save everyone else.

He stepped over to his station, putting in all of Cartwright's habits to date, Jacob got an idea of where he could be. Sealing every hatch in the three possible sections. Jacob sent security teams to capture all of the other groups from behind and then two details to each of the three sealed sections. He then opened a comm to the three sections with video sharing so that he could see which one Cartwright was in. "Eric Cartwright. This ends now." Cartwright's image was glaring back at him from the third section. Jacob quickly notified those Details while never looking away from the monster.

"Well, well, well. I finally get to see the face of Jacob Fallok. My popular nemesis behind all of this technology that's been fighting me. You know it's a shame you've been hiding from me this whole time. You've sent so many loved ones into my hands though, of course I can understand why you'd be afraid. Your eldest son, such a shame he killed himself before I could finish with him. Your brother though gave me quite a bit of fun until the very end. Why, even your wife and son-in-law died quite painfully I hear. Jack though, quite the fighter that boy is. Leading the team that took back Mar's Max. Smart of him to attack AFTER I left." The man said with a laugh. Jacob was visibly pissed and mortified. Melissa was nearby, when she started to approach, Jacob shied her away out of the camera's sight.

"I take it you're hiding your sweet little daughter near you?" Cartwright said with a knowing smile.

"This colony never did anything to hurt you Cartwright. Why attack it?" Jacob knew why but needed to keep him talking, to bide time for the security details to signal their readiness. Unfortunately, Cartwright saw through it.

"You're a smart man Fallok, you know why I'm here. The best offense is a good defense. Attacking Earth from here will mean sure victory. My only setback has been how well you've hidden yourself. Knowing to take over the colony I'd have to find your secret security compound. Congratulations though on all the preparations you went through for me. I'm honored I inspired you to make such drastic defensive and retreat preparations. Oh and there is just one thing I should inform you of. Those two security details at the door. They're my men, not yours. We fooled your sensors by taking the transponders. If you want to end this Fallok, you need to come here and end it with me. Face to Face.

You know where I am. Just introduce yourself to my detail outside, and let yourself in." With another belly laugh, Eric Cartwright shot the camera he was looking at, effectively cutting the transmission.

Locking up his console, Jacob turned to his daughter. "Daddy, don't go. He's lying to you."

"I know."

"He's just going to torture and kill you."

"I know."

"Once you're gone, it's all over for us."

"I know."

"Daddy, please don't go! I don't want to lose you!"

"I know."

"Daddy, I was going to wait until this was over, but I'm pregnant. Rich and I are going to be parents." This stopped Jacob just as he had gotten to the door. All stations had stopped what they were doing to watch the scene happening before them. Jacob turned around to face Melissa. She ran up to him and the two embraced in a hug. And he whispered in her ear.

"I didn't know. And I'm so proud of you. I will be back. But this has to get done. I love you sweetheart." He kissed her on the cheek, turned and walked away, signaling Commander Lee to come with him.

As the two walked quickly to the elevator, Jacob began telling her the plan and what she needed to get done in the time it would take him to get to Cartwrights location.

CHAPTER 31

Lieutenant Finnery was standing guard at the entrance way. Why though, he wasn't sure. General Cartwright and his team were trapped inside with no way out and the security team couldn't get in. So why stand guard.

Suddenly, a man approached the section, he wasn't alone either, there seemed to be two men with him. Raising his gun and taking aim at the leader. "Halt! State your name, affiliation and purpose!" Finnery called out.

The men just kept approaching. Finnery pulled the trigger on his gun and nothing happened. A second later, the man collapsed along with all of the men around him. As the three men approached Finnery, the leader knelt down, took a pulse of Finnery and stood back up. Hitting a button on his wrist controller, an influx of oxygen came into the section. He took a reading of the air and removed his breathing mask.

"Air is fine now. That was an effective gas you developed Rob. Nice EM burst to his gun too." Jacob said over the comm, knowing Rob was watching back at HQ. Turning to the other two men with him, Jacob asked, "Ready to go in?"

Jack and Tyler removed their breathing masks and had very determined stares. "Let's get this over with," Jack said.

With that, they approached the door, Rob opened it and they went in. Rob sealed it again as soon as they were inside and signaled Lee to commence moving the troops into the surrounding areas.

Jacob couldn't shake Tyler and Jack when they found out what he was doing. Apparently, Mel had called Jack up as soon as Jacob left the bunker and they were just arriving at the colony after their success at Mars Max. Before he even knew what hit him, the two were there.

Now, standing trapped in this room, 3-against-5, bad odds for them. Thank goodness for Rob otherwise this would be really bad. The three men looked at their adversary. "I'm here, Cartwright. Let's end this."

Cartwright stared at Jacob, then nodded towards Jack and Tyler. "What happened to coming alone?"

Looking to his family, Jacob smiled and looked back to Cartwright. "This is my home, and in my home, no matter how hard I may try, I am never alone. And I hope that never changes."

"How sweet. That sounds so lovey dovey for you. But this, this is war, you came here to surrender, and my condition was that you come alone. Your surrender is the only way to end this. My men are prepared to fight you to the end, and if we actually do fail to win, we will destroy this colony. My forces in space have the colony in their sights, if I don't live past this meeting, your colony doesn't either."

Jacob yawned, then turned to Jack and nodded. Jack activated his holo-monitor and showed the destruction of the Hawkeye fleet and lines of Hawkeyes being escorted thru Mars Max by the guards. Followed by the roundup of Hawkeyes all around Frontier and a recording just taken of the elimination of Cartwright's details outside the room. Jacob had kept his eyes on Cartwright the entire time. "It's over, Eric, you've lost. Please, stop the bloodshed."

Eric looked at the video, seeing all of his efforts going to hell. He saw there really wasn't anything left but suicide or capture. He swore never to become a prisoner of war and would be damned if he had to break that promise. So death it would be, but not alone.

Watching Cartwright like a hawk, Tyler saw the grenade just as his hands slipped to it, running in to stop him, Tyler struck Cartwright but too late to stop the pin from getting pulled. The two men toppled to the ground and the grenade went flying. It hit the ceiling and came back fast hitting the two men and exploding.

The whole room went up, Jack jumped over his father to protect him from the blast. And then darkness covered them all.

✳ ✳ ✳

Jack opened his eyes, looking up, he noticed the white clean ceiling, he turned his head and saw a bed with a man in it, and a girl sitting in a chair sleeping. She sat between the two beds. As his vision began to clear, he could make out his sister. The man in the bed was his father. It took a moment but he remembered what happened. Then he remembered about Tyler. He had to know. "Mel!" He said, his voice was hoarse, how long had it been since he spoke? She looked up, turned and saw him. She jumped from their dad's bed to his.

"Jack, thank goodness you're awake! How do you feel?" She began to cry as she hugged him. It looked like she had been crying a lot. But he had to know.

"Mel, what happened to Tyler and Cartwright?" The look in her face said everything. His co-pilot, best friend, and mentor was dead. Saving the lives of him and his father and killing the man who did all of this. Jack couldn't be brave anymore. He began crying, crying like never before. His brother was dead, mother and brother in law missing, his dad and him in the hospital, and Tyler was dead. And it was all finally over.

As Melissa watched her big brother cry, she for once was the strong one, she held him as he let it all out. She was happy it was over for him. Now she wanted Richard back. And just as she thought of him, another first happened. For the first time in history, the planet shook. The whole planet shook as a great internal force moved.

CHAPTER 32

Deep under the Martian surface, as the research team was moving about, Richard found the pattern in the map he was making. The underground city formed a pattern in its construction, through that pattern, he found the capital complex. Turning to his radio, "Team 2, I found the central complex. Sending coordinates to you for rendezvous." Richard walked up to the complex and entered. The architecture of this building was very different from the others. Large, raised, pillars that reminded him of Ancient Rome.

As he entered, he looked around, shining his light, he found symbols on the walls, different from the others places he had been. He followed the writings, up a stair case, down a corridor. Then he heard a voice. "I'm up here! Just follow the writings," he yelled back to those who had just entered.

Richard kept going, he found himself at a circular room, and began placing floor lights, he found the main chamber. Jessica and the others arrived just as Richard was setting up the last floor light. As he turned the lights on, he heard a gasp from behind him. He looked up and saw not a wall, but a being. Startled by the sight, Richard fell backwards. "What is that?" He asked.

Jessica just stood in awe, looking at it. Finally she said, "I think we just found proof of life on Mars."

Kevin took a step closer to the creature. "It obviously seems to be mammalian, humanoid of course, it has a lot of characteristics of a human and ape. We may be offshoots of them." Turning back to his colleagues, Kevin asked, "Do you think it could still be alive after all this time?" By now, Richard was back on his feet, looking at the helpless being stuck behind glass.

"It hasn't decomposed, but there isn't any power running in here, otherwise we would have lights, right? It must have died from power outage, and was just preserved well from the sterile environment," Jessica said.

Richard inched closer to the creature as he asked, "Is this even glass?" He rose his hand up and went to feel the glass. He touched the pane, and immediately was shocked. Lights and walls lit up all over the city. Oxygen began pouring into the city from vents all across the city. The glass began to melt around the creature and Richard dropped to the ground. Everyone screamed including the newly awakened being. Everyone except that is, for Richard Granit who now lay at the feet of the first awakened Martian in six billion years, dead.

A moment later, the entire city shook, throughout the city, thousands of chambers powered up, awakening those that were slumbering for eons. The Martians were back.

To be continued in Space Age Chronicles, Book 2: The Old System

Back story of Martian colony, separation of Earth and colonies.

Jacob Fallok - the Chief Executive Officer for Frontier Technologies and Second in Charge on the Colonial Board of Frontier Colony, the governing body for this colony. He was one of the co-founders of Frontier Colony 24 years earlier and his three children, wife, mother, and father all came to help set up the third Martian colony. His company provided key funding and plans for the Lunar and Martian Colonies in addition to the various space stations orbiting all of Earth, Luna and Mars. His sister, Jasmine Fallok, is the Chief Scientist on the primary lunar colony, Luna City.

Frontier Colony has a population of nearly 250,000 and was mostly underground with multiple Domes covering the surface with vast farms and a military base and a new wing recently opened to provide housing for an additional 20,000 prison guards, construction workers, miners, families, and schools. Located at the north canyon of the Valles Marineris.

Mars Maximum Penitentiary and Transfer Hub was located just 600 Kilometers next to the northeast end of the colony. As such, it was up to Frontier Colony to house the guards and their families. The Construction workers and miners were those on their six month break from construction on 10 Hygeia or nearby other Asteroid mines. When not mining in the Belt, they mined here on Mars; likewise for the construction workers.

With the growing shortage of natural resources on Earth, Mars had tons of resources of its own and was still being studied. An even better source of metallic resources was found to be in the Asteroid belt between Mars and Jupiter.

10 Hygeia, being one of the larger asteroids, had more metal on it than twice that of Earth in its prime and was unanimously deemed worthy to become the Ultimate Maximum Security Prison for life term inmates only. They would be responsible for growing their own food as well as mining the metals on 10 Hygeia to a safe level. Families were moved to Mars and each miner and guard worked on a six month shift; six months in the Belt and six months on Mars.

APPENDIX B
The Cartwright Manifesto

Hello, and welcome to the 42nd Rangers, also known as the Hawkeye Battalion. If you are reading this document, you have been cleared for this top secret file and welcomed into our ranks. Remember, secrecy is a must given the current state of global policies and this is a top secret document.

I am Lieutenant Colonel Eric Cartwright, the Hawkeye commanding officer. This is a collective of the current state of humanity in this ever changing ecosphere that we live and operate in as well as some solutions to help it live on as well as to save the planet that has spawned us.

As sworn members of the United Earth Peace Keeping Force, we have pledged an oath to protect humanity from itself across the planet as well as the interests of the United Earth Government.

You may have heard of me prior to joining our ranks due to some of our mission reports and battle. During the Third Korean War when Kim Jong Un IV launched a hack attack followed by a Nuclear Implosive missile at Seol, South Korea. My battalion went into Pyongyang to take out the ruthless dictator as well as his whole family. They decimated the South Korean government, so we took out the North Korean one. Now you have One Korea, reunited after nearly two hundred years at each others throats. They are policed by the UEPKF and have been given a government to answer to the UE government.

While we managed to fix a two hundred year problem, it came at a huge price. But the real question is, what was that price? Was it the loss of life on both sides? The breakdown of governments and leaders and walls? The generations of Koreans that will suffer from the radiation? Or the planet that is being scared by these nuclear bombs?

Throughout the short life that humanity has inhabited our mother Earth, we have constantly been poised to fight among ourselves. This isn't just us though. Wherever you have life, you have death. It is a balancing act of nature to prevent any species from over populating and consuming more resources than Gaia can provide.

Though this is a galactic constant, I'm keeping this document contained to Earth, at least for the time being.

At every point in our known history, one segment of our population has always been at war trying to conquer the rest of our species. Today our entire species has been conquered by one governing body, but it didn't take a shot, an arrow, a spear, a bomb. It only took an ideal. A single ideal managed to unite our planet under one body of rule.

That ideal was this, "We are facing a manmade extinction level event as we have delved too deeply into our planet's resource reservoir to safely repair it, we have grown so large our planet can barely sustain us, and our elders and their elders wasted too much time plundering our planet before they began trying to rectify what they had done that it is now too late for us."

This is all quite true. But there is a solution and while we have made great strides in reversing the damage caused by our industrialized explosion at the turn of the millennium, we still face many problems today by terrorists, eco-terrorists, greed, stubbornness to see the truth, and stupidity.

If you look into our history, really delve deep into the evolution of humanity from the past 6000 years of at least written language, you can see what has truly protected humanity from itself. But allow me to explain it clearly for you here.

Over the millennia we have walked this great Earth, there has always been something or someone to prevent humanity from growing too big too fast. The Romans, the Egyptians, the Persians all went around conquering the cowardly and slaughtering the brave. Then the church came about and gave us the crusades. Granted most of this was almost always towards the Jews, but others suffered as well. Then the black plague, Polio, warfare, revolutions, civil wars.

Natural disasters have been just as manacing as well to humanity. That alone shows mother nature is doing her best to keep us down. But humanity are like cochroaches. Every time humanity got knocked down it came back bigger, stronger, and smarter.

Even when you go into World Wars 1 and 2 and 3, Two especially you saw nearly a billion people die. But what happened by the end of the 20th century? Two hundred years of wars throughout the planet, billions killed between warfare, drug cartels, gangs, and petty crimes, but humanity was still bigger than ever with almost 8 BILLION people on our small planet. That was a hundred years ago. A hundred years before that, there was 1.6 Billion people on this planet. A 6.5 Billion person growth in a hundred years vs. the 5800 years before that.

No wonder our planet is failing us now if that's what it was a hundred years ago and today we are at 12 Billion people. Now you might be saying, hey, at least we aren't 16 or 20 billion like you might expect given those variables. But there is a reason for that. ASIDE from the nearly 1 Billion people you have living off planet (which brings us up to 13 Billion) We have very strict birthing limits worldwide now.

The problem though is that even at 8 billion, it was too much for the planet. So the question comes up, how do you cut down a population of 13 Billion down to a manageable number such as 5 or 6 Billion? That a more than 50% reduction in population, how do you do that?

Simple really, the 1 Billion off world have been banned from moving back to Earth. So you're down to 12 now to deal with.

Secondly, the third world nations that have terrorism and refuse to yield to the World Congress and keep popping out babies to suck up our oxygen need to be neutralized.

Third, if you do not have the skills to help us rejuvenate our planet or don't want to help, you should be neutralized.

Fourth, every country should have a lottery to decide which couples get to have 1 baby, and only half of the population are allowed to procreate.

While these are quite harsh I do admit, they are necessary to bring us back down to mid 20th century numbers within a generation, as well as help foster a stronger united planet.

As for the 1 Billion in space, I have not forgotten about them. You may ask, why do they get off the hook? They don't. The colonies have committed the worse crimes against humanity. They live richly off of the resources we provided to get them started. They do not adhere to the One child per family laws that we must abide by. And they would take the opportunity were our population to dwindle, to try and come back to Earth with their large and spoiled families.

This is why all of the 1 Billion people out in space should be left stuck out there or neutralized to prevent them from striking us down.

I thank you for taking the time to read this and am happy to welcome you into the fold as we prepare to bring Humanity back to a level where we can properly save our planet that has done so much for us.

Lt. Colonel Eric Cartwright
42nd Rangers
Hawkeye Battalion
UEPKF

A man sitting in the manmade
lake fishing, enjoying the nature
around him, It wasn't real but
it was close enough for mass.
Noticing no one was around he
decided he'd survived enough, he
deserved it. He pulled out a cigar
and enjoyed relaxing waiting for
a bite.

to be continued...

jsplevi@gmail.com
Josh Levi